Meinem Vater
Kraft Eberhard von Maltzahn
1925–2013

Johann Wolfgang von Goethe

Faust

The First Part
of the Tragedy

Johann Wolfgang von Goethe

Faust

The First Part of the Tragedy

Translated, with an Introduction and Notes,
by Margaret Kirby

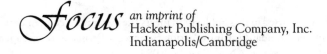 an imprint of
Hackett Publishing Company, Inc.
Indianapolis/Cambridge

Related Titles from the Focus Philosophical Library

Dante: Inferno ◆ T. Simone ◆ 2007
Dante: Purgatorio ◆ T. Simone ◆ 2014

A Focus Book

ℱocus an imprint of
 Hackett Publishing Company

Copyright © 2015 by Hackett Publishing Company, Inc.

18 17 16 15   1 2 3 4 5 6 7

For further information, please address
 Hackett Publishing Company, Inc.
 P.O. Box 44937
 Indianapolis, Indiana 46244-0937

 www.hackettpublishing.com

Cover image: Tissot, *Faust and Marguerite in the Garden* (1861).
Cover design adapted from design by Guy Wetherbee | Elk Amino Design,
New England | elkaminodesign@yahoo.com
Composition by William Hartman

Library of Congress Cataloging-in-Publication Data

Goethe, Johann Wolfgang von, 1749–1832, author.
  [Faust. 1. Theil. English]
  Faust : the first part of the tragedy / Johann Wolfgang von Goethe ;
  Translated, with an Introduction and Notes, by Margaret Kirby.
       pages cm
  Includes bibliographical references.
  ISBN 978-1-58510-740-7 (pbk.)
  1. Faust, –approximately 1540—Drama. I. Kirby, Margaret Anne,
  1956– translator. II. Title.
  PT2026.F2K57 2015
  832'.6—dc23   2015005286

Contents

ACKNOWLEDGEMENTS

I would like to thank those with whom I first read Goethe's *Faust*, Professor Detlev Steffen of Dalhousie University in Nova Scotia, Canada, and Professor Peter Michelsen of the University of Heidelberg. My thanks are also due to James Doull, in the Classics Department at Dalhousie, in whose classes I spent many hours reading and translating Homer and the Greek tragedians. Professor Hans Eichner, at the University of Toronto, encouraged my interest in Goethe and supervised my doctoral dissertation on Goethe's concept of *Tätigkeit*.

It is above all my colleagues and students at St. John's College who have helped me become a more attentive and thoughtful reader and translator. I've benefited from reading, discussing, and translating *Faust* with many students. I am especially grateful to those of my colleagues who participated in a summer study group on Goethe's concept of the natural phenomenon and to the Pettus-Crowe Foundation for funding that study group, as well as some release time from my teaching responsibilities.

I am grateful to Ron Pullins at Focus Publishing for first proposing this translation and want to extend my thanks to those at Hackett Publishing who took it over with such enthusiasm and have done so much to bring the project to fruition: Rick Todhunter, Laura Clark, and Harbour Fraser Hodder.

My mother, Anne von Maltzahn, has supported and encouraged me in countless ways over many years. Finally, I wish to extend my thanks and love to my daughters, Elizabeth and Kate, and my husband, Torrance, who do so much to sustain me.

An Introduction to *Faust I*

The Earthly Drama

We first encounter Faust sitting "restlessly" at his desk in a "narrow Gothic room" (SD 354).[1] It is night. Faust describes the study in which his scholarly pursuits have confined him as a gloomy "prison" (398) and depicts himself as a man incarcerated by towering stacks of books and papers, as well as by endless collections of scientific instruments and specimens. This metaphorical prison threatens to metamorphose into something even more sinister, as Faust remarks that his books are buried in dust and gnawed by worms, and complains that he is surrounded by "bones and skeletons," "soot and rot" (416–17). The academic world seems to him little more than a tomb.

Not only has learning failed to liberate Faust, but the scientific investigations that epitomize his intellectual endeavors have in fact distanced him further from the object of his inquiry; his analysis of nature has estranged him from the "living nature" he so desperately seeks to grasp (414). The difficulty seems to be, as the devil Mephistopheles playfully suggests later in the drama, that the student of nature, in his efforts to distinguish the constitutive parts of the natural world, inevitably destroys the living being that is the focus of his investigation (1936–39). The very experiments by means of which Faust thought to discover nature's secrets have slammed nature's "gate" firmly shut, while the instruments that were to have functioned as his "keys" have failed to lift nature's "latch" (670–71). Although the condition described here seems to be one of exile rather than imprisonment, the persistent imagery of gates and keys indicates that the confinement Faust feels is closely linked to his deep sense of exclusion from the natural world.[2]

---

1. SD indicates a stage direction; the number is that of the line immediately following the stage direction.

2. See also l. 1747: "Nature has locked me out."

The language in which Faust articulates his desire for knowledge is revealing. He insists that the knowledge that would free him from his ignorance is one that would allow him to drink directly from nature's breasts (456–59). The problem is that nature resists all his attempts to expose her, refusing to be "robbed" of her "veil" (672).[3] Unable to imagine any meaningful engagement with the natural world that would leave this veil intact, Faust announces that he has adopted an alternate path, hoping that magic will finally allow him to penetrate the veil and look directly at nature's "potencies and seeds" (384).[4] He hopes that this penetrating insight will enable him to escape the strictures of discursive reason and the bonds of an academic learning he now considers mere sophistry or "traffic in words" (385). Nonetheless, despite his talk of fleeing from his study "Out to open countryside" (418), Faust opens his books once more and, prompted by what he finds there, invokes the Earth Spirit. When the Earth Spirit rejects him, Faust contemplates suicide, imagining that the dissolution of the self will finally grant him the direct contact with nature he so intensely longs for and will allow him "To penetrate the ether," as his "unfettered powers / . . . flow through nature's veins" (704; 618–19). Faust's emphatic use of the first person singular in these passages, however, suggests that his acute self-awareness may be what poses the greatest barrier between self and world.[5]

The sound of the Easter bells evokes memories of the Christian faith Faust once possessed and calls him out of his study. The Easter hymn he hears celebrates a release from the "bonds" of death and corruption (800). Although Faust does not share the choir's faith, he feels restored by the sight of the reawakening natural world and the people who have come outside to celebrate. In the spring countryside he finds reflected a sense of liberation: "streams and brooks are freed of ice" (903), while the populace

---

3. The German verb *berauben* ("rob") contains the noun *Raub*—"theft" or "rape"—and is related to the English words "rob" and "rape." I have translated the verb as "tear" in order to convey the sense of violence suggested by *berauben*.

4. It may be helpful to note that because the German noun *Natur* ("nature") is feminine and must therefore be referred to by feminine pronouns, it is not always clear when nature is being personified.

5. See, for example, ll. 623–27 (my italics):
> I can't presume to claim that *I'm* your equal!
> Though *I* possessed the power to draw you,
> *I* had no power at all to keep you here.
> In that ecstatic moment,
> *I* felt so small and yet so great . . .

pours "Out of the dark and hollow gate" (918) of the city and breaks "Out" of the various "bonds" that held it there.[6]

Goethe recasts the pact with the devil, which lies at the heart of the traditional legend of Faust, as a wager. Faust's wager with Mephistopheles, which concludes what is roughly the first half of *Faust I*, suggests that Faust's feeling of confinement stems from an even deeper and more fundamental sense of captivity than the opening scene in his study reveals. Faust initially complained of his inability to escape his intellectual confines; at the heart of the wager lies the claim that he will never be able to escape the strictures of temporal existence—"The anguish of this narrow earthly life" (1545). To say "Stay a while" to the moment, or to see a moment as "fair" and beautiful, is to find something of lasting value in a particular, finite instant (1700). This, Faust wagers, is precisely what he can never and will never do. Nevertheless, the wager is at the same time a challenge to Mephistopheles, "the spirit that continually negates," to prove Faust wrong and to show him that there *is* something of substance in finitude (1338). While Faust clings desperately to the wager as his only remaining means of escape from despair, Mephistopheles revels in the certainty that Faust is inextricably bound to him, precisely because Faust is essentially dissatisfied with all forms of temporal existence:

> Fate has given him a spirit
> That presses on without restraint,
> Whose overhasty striving
> Overleaps all earthly joys. (1856–59)[7]

Gretchen, the name by which the character Margarete is usually known,[8] is trapped in a prison of a very different sort. Faust discovers in the confines of her "small tidy room" an atmosphere of tranquility, order, and contentment, which he finds liberating and even salvific—

---

6. Six lines begin with the preposition "Out" (ll. 918, 923, 924, 925, 926, and 927). In l. 924 Faust refers to "bonds of work and business."

7. The logic of Mephistopheles' argument is a bit confusing. What he says here about Faust's fundamental "overhastiness" would seem to ensure that it is Faust rather than Mephistopheles who will ultimately win the wager—Faust will never rest satisfied in the moment. Nevertheless, Mephistopheles' perception that Faust's *dis*satisfaction will also forever bind Faust to the spirit of negation seems entirely correct. Constant dissatisfaction is a form of constant negation.

8. At l. 2849 Faust asks, "And Gretchen?" Some scenes use the name Margarete, while others use Gretchen.

> Oh what abundance in this poverty!
> In this prison what salvation! (2693–94)

Yet Gretchen herself describes a rather narrow world governed by class structure and economic necessity:

> . . . in the end,
> All things depend on gold,
> Throng toward gold. Alas we poor! (2802–4)

Gretchen's speech is peppered with the adjectives "little" and "small"; like her name, many of the nouns she uses terminate in the German diminutive ending "–chen." Her neighbor Martha is the grotesque epitome of the pettiness of the social sphere in which Gretchen finds herself, although it is her brother Valentin who displays the darkest aspects of that world.

Near the beginning of her relation to Faust, Gretchen finds a "little box" (2783), which she unlocks with a "little key" (2788).[9] The action is symbolic. Although Gretchen in many ways embodies the very antithesis of Faust's "overhasty striving" (1858), it is important to note that he is able to enter and ultimately to shatter her world, because he appears to offer a way out of an existence that, especially now that her baby sister has died, seems repetitive and tedious—"Day in, day out the same" (3146). Gretchen's use of song and prayer as primary modes of expression suggests that she is securely housed in the culture and religion of her people, yet her attraction to Faust arises in part from a desire—albeit incipient and vague—to escape that world. At the same time, for Gretchen, Faust is attractive precisely because of the place he seems to occupy in that class-conscious society: she quickly persuades herself that he is a nobleman— "Yes, I could read it in his brow" (2682). Her endeavors to break out of her narrow domestic world end, of course, tragically. No sooner has she consummated her love for Faust than she experiences, as Lieschen gossips about "little Barbara"[10] and Barbara's pregnancy (3544–49), the terrible pettiness of town life, a pettiness to which, Gretchen now realizes, she herself has contributed. The church provides no relief: despite Gretchen's

---

9. It is worth noting that as Gretchen unlocks the box, her speech falls out of its previous tight four-foot iambic rhythm into the looser verse forms used by Faust and Mephistopheles. The structure of her lines also becomes looser; ll. 2792–93, for example, are strongly enjambed, in contrast to the end-stopped lines that initially characterize her speech.

10. I have anglicized the German name *Bärbelchen*. The German name *Bärbel* is itself a diminutive of Barbara, while the suffix *–chen* adds a further diminutive ending.

anguished prayer to the *Mater Dolorosa* at the city wall (3587–3619), the cathedral itself figures as a nightmarish prison, whose walls not only trap the pregnant Gretchen, but seem to close in on and threaten to crush her (3816–3820).

The closing scene of *Faust I* is titled "Prison." As the curtain rises, Faust is standing outside "a small iron door" holding "a bundle of keys," having come—with the help of Mephistopheles—to offer Gretchen a means of escape (SD 4405). As we gather from her song and her deranged musings, Gretchen has been imprisoned and sentenced to death for drowning her newborn child. Although she briefly perceives her beloved as a means of release—"I heard him calling. / I'm free!" (4462–63)—he figures as a release not from prison, but from the powers of hell, which, she is convinced, are "seething" right beneath the doorsill (4455–56).[11] Conflating— or confusing—literal and metaphorical realities, Gretchen is briefly able to see Faust as a means of redemption from "The Evil One" (4458). Nevertheless, she rejects Faust's insistence that they hurry away and asks him to stay with her, as she once stayed with him (4479–80). Her use of the verb *weilen* ("stay") echoes the verb *verweilen* ("stay a while") of Faust's wager (1700). Faust, however, characteristically intent on escape, cannot hear her and only insists more emphatically that she make haste. In her madness Gretchen sees clearly that there is no escape for her. She understands that she can no more escape the prison than she can escape the deeds she has committed: "Why flee? They'll only lie in wait for me" (4545). At the same time, the "Voice (from above)" that pronounces Gretchen's salvation—"Is saved!" (4611)—introduces a view of the action that differs radically from the perspective offered by Mephistopheles or any of the human participants in the drama. The dramatic struggle between Mephistopheles' last words to Faust—"Come here to me!" (4611)—and the "Voice (from within)" the prison that calls out "Heinrich! Heinrich!" (4612)[12] suggests that despite Faust's restless dissatisfaction and despite all the suffering he has caused, he himself may not ultimately belong to Mephistopheles.

11.   Her reference to "the voice of my friend" in l. 4461 reveals much about her vision of Faust at that moment: the phrase echoes Luther's translation of the Song of Solomon 2:8; Gretchen conflates Faust, the earthly bridegroom, with Christ, the heavenly bridegroom, who, according to Christian tradition (and particularly according to the Pietist tradition with which Goethe was very familiar), is metaphorically prefigured in the beloved of the Song of Solomon. See note to l. 4435.

12.   We learn that this is Faust's first name when Gretchen says, "Promise me, Heinrich," at l. 3414.

The "Prologue in Heaven"

At roughly the same time that Goethe was at work developing the scene of the pact between Faust and Mephistopheles (lines 1530–1769), he added the "Prologue in Heaven," which seems to cast the entire drama in a very different and considerably brighter light than our brief analysis of the earthly drama might suggest possible. As the archangels contemplate the motion of the sun and planets, they give voice to a view in which time does not function as a constraint, but as a moving image of eternity. The angelic hymn describes a kind of cosmic competition, in which the self-sustaining activity of the cosmos arises from the profound desire of each part to outdo the other, that is, to be the best at doing what it does. The hymn generates a tremendous sense of motion, which is underscored by the complete absence of any body that is at rest: while the motion ascribed to the sun in the opening lines suggests a geocentric model of the universe, the following stanza of the angelic hymn reveals that the earth is in motion as well, and indeed moves with "Incomprehensible" speed (251).[13] At the same time the hymn establishes a fundamental sense of constancy: despite or perhaps because of their ineffable motion, the divine works remain "glorious as on that first day" (250 and 270). From this archangelic perspective, temporal appearances do not veil or obscure, but reflect their original, timeless cause.

Mephistopheles' entry onto the stage, however, immediately affords us a very different—perhaps more comic than cosmic—perspective on the relentless activity of nature.[14] Against the macrocosmic backdrop, Mephistopheles introduces a human microcosm that is equally unchanging:

> The small god of the world persists in his old ways—
> Is as peculiar as on that first day. (281–82)

Mephistopheles' parody of the angelic refrain suggests that the cyclical activity of the natural world is pointless, and not so much an imitation of the divine as a comic inversion of God's self-sameness. What the angels, from their distant, macrocosmic perspective, interpret as constancy—"glorious

---

13.   It has been suggested that in avoiding both a geocentric Ptolemaic view *and* a heliocentric Copernican model, Goethe may have had in mind something like the astronomical system of the Pythagoreans, in which sun and earth orbit along with various other heavenly bodies around the common midpoint of a central fire (FA, part I, vol. 7.2, p. 165).

14.   It is not clear at precisely what point Mephistopheles comes on stage: the stage directions at the beginning of the Prologue note simply, "Later Mephistopheles" (SD 243). He seems at least to have overheard the end of the angelic hymn, which he parodies at l. 282.

as on that first day"—Mephistopheles, from his microcosmic standpoint, construes as an endless recurrence of the identical—"as peculiar as on that first day." Mephistopheles' viewpoint also reveals a world of endless activity, but this activity is now understood as movement that lacks any direction. From a diabolical perspective, human activity looks completely futile, because humanity shows absolutely no signs of progress. Mephistopheles likens man to a long-legged grasshopper whose motion seems the very embodiment of purposelessness:

> . . . He seems to me—
> Your Grace must pardon the analogy—
> Like one of those long-legged grasshoppers,
> That always fly and flying spring
> Into the grass and sing the same old song. (286–90)

What looked so grand from a macrocosmic perspective—the sun's ability to intone its ancient melody in harmony with the other planets—looks rather pathetic from this microcosmic standpoint: humans do nothing but sing the same old tune over and over again. Mephistopheles measures motion solely in terms of progress and, as he later admits, is frustrated by his inability to make any headway in his own destructive efforts:

> Through waves and storms, through quakes and fires—
> In the end both sea and land remain at rest! (1367–68)

Although here too his vocabulary echoes the angelic hymn, Mephistopheles once more inverts the angelic vision. Precisely what the angels perceive positively as nature's end—that is, to remain constantly "glorious as on that first day"—Mephistopheles regards negatively as inactivity and endless repetition with no sign of change.

It is Mephistopheles' portrait of humans as unambitious grasshoppers that apparently provokes the Lord to bring up his "servant" Faust (299). What Mephistopheles classifies as madness, however, the Lord calls service, and what Mephistopheles classifies as discontent, the Lord refers to as striving (317). In a strange twist on the story of Job, it is apparently *not* because Faust is "perfect and upright"[15] that this Lord has such confidence in his servant, but because Faust is endlessly dissatisfied. Complacency is, so the Lord proposes, the greatest threat to man's salvation, while constant

---

15. Job 1:1. All quotations from the Bible are taken from the Authorized (King James) Version (AKJV).

*dis*satisfaction, that is to say, a continual rejection or negation of the finite, implicitly insists that man is not truly at home in the finite world. Insofar as man contends with time, or strives, he expresses the conviction that what he is really after differs fundamentally from the finitude he experiences. Because Mephistopheles is a spirit of perpetual negation, the Lord claims that this "rogue who scoffs" (339) ultimately functions as an instrument of redemption. Thus, paradoxically, Faust's insistent dissatisfaction both binds him to Mephistopheles *and* provides the surest guarantee that Faust is *not* finally of the devil's party. Nonetheless, although negation thus appears to function, *sub specie aeternitatis*, as an affirmative force, it has, from a human standpoint, the most tragic consequences, as Gretchen's tragedy makes all too clear. The Lord urges the "true sons of God" (344) to adopt a different approach to the phenomenal world. He exhorts the angels to respond to the wavering appearances that embrace them in "gentle bonds of love" (347) not by trying to shake off those bonds, but by affirming and securing the appearances "with enduring thoughts" (349). His exhortation invites us to ask whether this affirmative path is restricted to angelic intellects or is also open to human beings.

The "Prelude in the Theater" and "Dedication"

Grand as the cosmic vision of the Prologue is, we should, nonetheless, bear in mind that the preceding "Prelude in the Theater" presents the heavenly prologue as a staged event. By introducing the ensuing action as a spectacle performed in a "narrow house of boards" (239) and the theater itself as a commercial enterprise, the Prelude threatens to undermine even the Lord's authority. In the Prelude, the "Director" reminds the "Dramatic Poet" and the "Comic Actor" that their theatrical venture is dependent on the whims of the people, who, desperate to escape their boredom (*Langeweile*), satiety, and addiction to the popular press (113–16), struggle to squeeze "through the narrow gate" (51) leading into the theater.[16] Just like their other pastimes—card games, newspapers, and a "wild night" (126)—the theatrical spectacle serves the people as a diversion and escape from the demands of daily existence. In the words of the Director, idealistic poets who refuse to acknowledge the appetites of their audience are simply "poor fools" (127).

Nevertheless, while the Prelude presents the whole drama as "merely a spectacle" (454), it is helpful to bear in mind that the "Dedication" that precedes the Prelude offers some assurance that *Faust I* is more than mere

---

16.   A parody of Luke 13:24. See note to l. 51.

illusion.[17] In contrast to the Poet of the Prelude, who is constrained by the dictates of popular taste as well as by the Director who employs him, the poet of the Dedication suggests that the "forms" (1, *Gestalten*) that occupy his poetic imagination, inconstant though they may be, have an existence and life that is independent not only of the exigencies of daily life, but also of the poet's own attempts to "hold" them "fast" (3).[18] The use of reflexive forms in the opening stanza of the Dedication implies that the "fluctuating forms" themselves are ultimately the authors of their own appearance in a particular time and place.[19] The poet suggests that it is they who govern him, rather than the other way around. The word "Dedication" (*Zueignung*) itself leaves open the possibility that the poet is not so much dedicating his poem to someone, as giving himself over to the fluctuating forms that seem to appropriate his attention. It is when the poet yields, or dedicates himself to them, that what he initially dismisses as mere "illusions" (4) become "realities" (32) for him.

Fluctuating Forms

In contrast to the "overhasty striving" (1858) that characterizes Faust's approach to the world, the "eternal speed" (258) the archangel Gabriel ascribes to the cosmos does not spring from dissatisfaction with finitude. The archangels present the cosmic movements as a form of imitation, by means of which finite phenomena reflect the infinitude—the eternity—of their underlying cause. By associating temporal motion with eternity, the archangels suggest that the cosmic phenomena they contemplate arise from a synthesis of the polarity between finite and infinite. Faust's wager with Mephistopheles, on the other hand, denies the possibility of such a synthesis, because it denies the very possibility that a transient moment can contain meaning. In Gretchen's room, Faust has a momentary vision of a fusion of the two realms he insists on separating, an intimation that an earthly

---

17. The word *Schauspiel*, composed from the nouns *Schau* ("show") and *Spiel* ("game"), means both "drama" and "spectacle."

18. Goethe's poetry is informed by the same principle of *wiederholte Spiegelungen* ("repeated mirrorings" or "repeated reflections"), which he regarded as constitutive of natural organisms. The poet's use of the verb *festhalten* ("hold fast") is perhaps reflected in the Lord's use of the verb *befestigen* ("fasten" or "secure") in his final command to the angels (349): "Make steadfast with enduring thoughts." There is certainly a long tradition that claims poets are the gods' "true sons."

19. For example, the beginning of the first line more literally reads, "You bring yourselves near (*Ihr naht euch*) again," and the fifth line could be translated, "You thrust yourselves (*Ihr drängt euch*) closer."

"prison" can contain meaning or "salvation": "In this prison what salvation!" (2694). It is not, however, a vision Faust can sustain, because its ground is entirely subjective: his vision reflects his own romantic notion of Gretchen's life and simply "Overleaps" (1859) the realities of Gretchen's world.

Goethe himself considers "overhastiness" one of the distinguishing features but also one of the greatest dangers of modern life.[20] He cautions the observer of nature, for example, to "guard against every overhastiness" and lists "impatience" and "haste" (*Vorschnelligkeit*) among the "inner enemies" that constitute the greatest danger to the student of nature.[21] Against this Goethe recommends that we abandon our insistent attempts to remove nature's veils and that we cultivate a habit of "calm attention" (*ruhige Aufmerksamkeit*) to the phenomena.[22] Although it is only in Part Two of *Faust* that Goethe considers more fully the political effects of modern man's "overhastiness," *Faust I* suggests that by dedicating ourselves more attentively to the world's constantly shifting appearances—its "fluctuating forms"—we may begin to find paths that liberate us.

A Note on the Text

Goethe's *Faust* is a drama whose own form fluctuated somewhat. In 1887 a manuscript, which seems to be a copy of the very earliest form of Goethe's Faust drama, was discovered and published with the title *Goethe's Faust in Its Original Form*. It is now known as the *Urfaust*. It is the fruit of

---

20. Goethe coined the term *veloziferisch* ("velociferous") to describe what he called "the greatest evil of our time, which lets nothing come to fruition." The coinage echoes the French noun *vélocifère* (a fast stage-coach), but also ominously couples the Latin word *velox* with the name Lucifer to evoke the diabolical haste Goethe found so pernicious. WA, part I, vol. 42.2, p. 171.

21. Goethe, "The Experiment as Mediator between Object and Subject," WA, part II, vol. 11, pp. 23 and 28. Goethe repeatedly returns to this theme: "Theories are usually the overhastiness (*Übereilungen*) of an impatient understanding, which would like to rid itself of the phenomena as quickly as possible" (Goethe, *Maxims and Reflections*, #548, HA 12, p.440); cf. also #550: "If we consider Aristotle's *aporiai* or problems, we are astonished by the gift for observation and by how many things the Greeks had an eye for. But they make the mistake of overhastiness (*Übereilung*), insofar as they proceed directly from the phenomenon to the explanation, and in this way unsatisfactory theoretical pronouncements arise. This, however, is the general mistake that is still being made today."

22. Goethe, "The Experiment as Mediator . . . , p. 22. The quality of "calm attentiveness" is a crucial one for Goethe. It is one of the features that distinguishes Ottilie, a central character in his novel *Elective Affinities*, and enables her to resist being drawn into the urgent and ultimately destructive landscaping projects that absorb the other characters in that novel. WA, part I, vol. 20, p. 69; cf. also p. 113.

Goethe's work on *Faust* between 1772 and 1775, and includes—almost unchanged—the opening scene in Faust's study and—in prose form—the concluding scene in prison. Goethe does not seem to have worked on *Faust* again until 1788. In 1790 he published *Faust: A Fragment*. In this version the drama also opens with the initial scene in Faust's study, but it concludes with the scene "Cathedral." Many of the prose scenes from *Urfaust* now appear in verse form, and the scenes "Witch's Kitchen" and "Forest and Cave" are new. *Faust I*, or properly speaking, *Faust: The First Part of the Tragedy*, appeared in 1808 and included several major additions: a long section that includes most of the pact scene (606–1769), which seems to have been part of Goethe's original conception of the drama, and the three prefatory pieces ("Dedication," "Prelude in the Theater," and "Prologue in Heaven"). Although Goethe had already begun writing a second part of the drama in 1800, much of the second part was written in the final years of his life. *Faust: The Second Part of the Tragedy* was not published until 1833, a year after Goethe's death.

A Note on the Translation

> And then I saw that my exalted flight—
> As it had seemed to me—was merely the endeavor
> Of a worm down in the dust, which sees an eagle
> Soaring toward the sun and yearns to rise
> Like it. It strives to climb and twists and turns,
> And timidly strains every nerve, and still
> Remains there in the dust.[23]

Every translator is familiar with the frustration Faust expresses as he tries to translate the first verse of John's Gospel. As he attempts to "translate / This sacred text" into his "beloved German" (1221–23), Faust impatiently dismisses every alternative as inadequate to the task. He quickly realizes that no German word is able to convey the manifold sense of the Greek word *logos*. Even the most patient translator is all too aware that the "best" translation is at times only the least of numerous evils, none of which quite captures the many possible implications of the original. At the same time, every reader of a translation is familiar with the experience that Don Quixote compares to looking at a tapestry from the wrong side: the figures

---

23. From a letter Goethe wrote to his friend Johann Jacob Riese, April 28, 1766. (At the time, Goethe was a sixteen-year-old university student in Leipzig.) WA, part IV, vol. 1, p. 46.

are visible, but threads and knots obscure "the smoothness and color of the right side."[24] Paradoxically enough, it can be just the translator's zealous attachment to individual words that gives rise to the reader's impression of looking at the back of a canvas: Quixote dismisses the translator as a person who says "pleases" where the Tuscan says *piace*, "more" where it says *più*, and who renders *su* as "above" and *giù* as "below." The translator is compelled to navigate between the seductive but generally illusory notion of literal translation, and the idea that some sort of fidelity to the sense of the original gives him license to ignore the actual words of the text.

The following translation attempts to be precise without being formulaic. While it is important to know when and where a word or phrase is repeated, the simple equation of a German term *x* with an English term *y* is of course frequently misleading. For example, both Faust and his all-too-scholarly assistant Wagner use the word *Geist*. But what Faust understands by this word, when he claims that he feels Gretchen's "spirit [*Geist*] / Of order and abundance wafting round" him (2702–3), is not what Wagner means, when he claims that "Everyone would like to know a bit about" the "human heart and mind [*Geist*]" (586–87). In this instance the German word encompasses what we, with our two distinct words "spirit" and "mind," regard as two quite different meanings. At the same time, it is critical that the reader be aware of the way a word begins to disclose its import as it appears in different settings. The word "wager" (*Wette*), for instance, first appears in the "Prologue in Heaven." The archangel Raphael describes the sun and planetary spheres as engaged in a great song-competition (*Wettgesang*, 244), while Gabriel attributes a more contentious rivalry to the roaring storm-winds (*Stürme brausen um die Wette*, 259). These cosmic rivalries seem to have little to do with the wager (*Wette*) Mephistopheles offers the Lord later in the same scene (312) and even less with the wager Faust offers Mephistopheles almost 1500 lines later (1698). Nevertheless, the suggestion that a wager of sorts underlies the regular motion of the sun and planets, as well as the noisy commotion of the storm-winds, invites us to ask whether Faust's wager bears some relation to all this cosmic competition. Occasionally the verbal echoes seem almost too faint or too distant to be significant. For example, Valentin's "You can bet on that!" (*Topp! Topp!* 3634) repeats the expression Mephistopheles uses in accepting Faust's wager some 2000 lines earlier (1698). Valentin's image of the soldiers' drunken rivalry offers only the

---

24. Miguel de Cervantes, *Don Quixote*, trans. Edith Grossman (New York : Harper Collins, 2003), part II, chapter 62, p. 873.

palest shadow of the great wager that expresses Faust's endless dissatisfaction with our time-bound existence. Yet inattention to these verbal threads obscures the ways Faust's dissatisfaction is embedded in a universal competitive urge that drives not only the behavior of man and devil, but the activity of the cosmos itself.

Critical as it is to attend to questions of vocabulary, language, especially the language of a dramatic poem such as *Faust*, consists of many other elements. Some of these features make *Faust* a drama, others make it a poem. Different characters speak in different voices—we have already noted a contrast between Faust and the pedantic Wagner. Gretchen's voice, paradoxically, is distinctive by not being distinct—she expresses herself most profoundly in words that are not her own but the words of folksong and folktale, or the words of the Church and scriptures. Mephistopheles, too, often adopts the words and voices of others, but he appropriates in order to parody. He is a wonderful mimic: his impersonation of Faust and explanation of the various academic faculties to a newly arrived student is simply very funny. One of the greatest challenges for the translator is to find Faust's voice, while at the same time conveying the vast scope of his character and the dramatic shifts of his mood and emotions. To add to the difficulty, although the drama was published in 1808 as *Faust: The First Part of the Tragedy*, it is infused with comic scenes and characters, so that tragic and comic registers often seem strangely blended.

The translator of *Faust I* faces an additional set of obstacles. The drama is remarkable for its tremendous metrical range. Its verse forms include the majestic rhymed hymnic stanzas of the "Prologue in Heaven"; a doggerel-like form known as *Knittelvers*, usually in rhymed couplets, in which four stressed syllables are combined with an irregular number of unstressed syllables; and the dominant meter of *Faust I*, called "madrigal verse," in which stressed and unstressed syllables alternate regularly, but the number of feet per line and the rhyme scheme vary. A single scene can encompass diverse metrical forms, as can even a single speech: after the archangels' hymn, Mephistopheles begins to speak in iambic pentameter, using alternating rhymes that echo the archangels' rhyme scheme (271–78). He then slips into madrigal verse, incorporating a pair of alexandrines (lines of six feet with a *caesura* or break in the middle) as he begins his description of the human race (281–82). Likewise, a single character can speak in a great variety of verse forms. Faust himself is striking in this respect: his great monologue at the beginning of the "Forest and Cave" scene is couched in blank verse (3217–50), his speech in the pact scene is in a tightly controlled four-foot iambic meter, while his emotional confession of faith in "Martha's Garden" lapses into free rhythms, to list just a few examples.

These metrical qualities are closely linked to other formal aspects of the drama, which also contribute to its endlessly shifting registers of tone. Mephistopheles' fast-paced and sardonic humor and preference for Latinate vocabulary are a far cry from the predominantly Germanic and often monosyllabic voice in which Gretchen gives utterance to her inmost feelings. On the whole, however, the language and style of *Faust I* are quick and direct. This is partly the effect of its syntax, which tends to avoid the use of subordinate clauses and to favor paratactic structures, in which parallel clauses are simply set beside each other or joined by "and." Lines of verse are predominantly end-stopped. When characters do speak in enjambed lines it is often significant: the enjambed line and verse structure in the last eight lines of the song Gretchen sings at her spinning wheel makes her longing and loss of equilibrium audible and almost palpable (3406–13).

The present translation attempts to balance these various demands. It strives to convey the text as carefully as possible to the contemporary English reader, while also trying to echo something of the marvelous language and many tones of *Faust I*. The endeavor throughout has been not only to bring the drama into the reader's world but also to bring the reader into the world of the drama, with the hope that worlds which seemed far from us will, in the words of Goethe's "Dedication," "become realities."

Editions Cited (*All translations from the German are my own.*)

Goethes Werke (Hamburger Ausgabe). Edited by Erich Trunz. Ninth edition. Munich: Beck, 1981. (Abbreviated as HA.)

Goethes Werke (Weimarer Ausgabe). Weimar: Böhlau, 1887–1919. (Abbreviated as WA.)

Sämtliche Werke (Frankfurter Ausgabe). Frankfurt: Deutscher Klassiker Verlag, 1985-99. (Abbreviated as FA.)

Dedication

Once more you draw near, fluctuating forms
That early on appeared to my dim gaze.
Shall I then try to hold you fast this time?
Is my heart still inclined to those illusions?
You're thronging toward me now! Then have your way,   5
As you rise round me out of mist and fog;
My breast is shaken with a youthful feeling
By the magic breath that drifts about your path.

You bring with you the scenes of happy days,
And many a beloved shadow rises;   10
First love and friendship surface with them,
Just like some old and half-forgotten tale;
Sorrow revives, and my lament retraces
The labyrinthine, wandering path of life
And names good friends, who, robbed of lovely hours   15
By fortune's tricks, have vanished from my sight.

They will not hear the following songs,
Those souls to whom I sang the first;
That throng of friends is scattered now,
And that first echo too has died away.   20
My song[1] sings to an unknown multitude,
And even their applause alarms my heart,

---

1. Some editions read *Leid* ("suffering") here, rather than *Lied* ("song"). This was probably a typographical error in the first edition.

While all who once delighted in my verses
Wander the world dispersed, if they're alive.

A long-forgotten yearning seizes me   25
For that quiet, solemn realm of spirits;
In indefinite tones my whispering song
Floats in the air, like an Aeolian harp;
A shuddering comes over me, tear follows tear,
My rigid heart feels soft and mild;   30
All I possess seems far away from me;
Things that were gone become realities.

Prelude in the Theater

(Director. Dramatic Poet. Comic Actor.)

Director. You two who have so often stood
            By me in times of need and trouble,
            What do you think the prospects are   35
            For our enterprise, now we're on German ground?
            I do so want to please the multitude—
            It lives and lets live, as you know.
            The posts and boards have been erected,
            And everyone's expecting quite a feast.   40
            They're sitting there, eyes open wide,
            Relaxed and ready for a real surprise.
            I know what's popular these days,
            And yet I've never been at such a loss:
            The people aren't accustomed to the best,   45
            But still, they've read an awful lot.
            What shall we do, so all is fresh and new,
            Significant, but entertaining too?
            To tell the truth, I like to see the multitude
            Thronging and streaming toward our stage   50
            And squeezing through the narrow gate of grace[2]

---

2.   A parody of Luke 13:24: "Strive to enter in at the strait gate: for many, I say unto you, will seek to enter in, and shall not be able." All quotations from the Bible are taken from the Authorized (King James) Version (AKJV).

With strong, recurrent labor-pains.
In broad daylight, well before four,
They shove and fight to reach the ticket-booth;
Like starving beggars at a baker's door,   55
They'd break their necks to get a ticket.
Only a poet can work such wonders
On such a mix of people; my friend, work one today!

Poet.   Don't speak about that gaudy multitude,
At the sight of which the spirit flees us.   60
Conceal from me the surging, swelling throng
That pulls us in its wake against our will.
Lead me instead to quiet heavenly confines,
For there alone pure joy blooms for the poet,
And there, with godlike hands, love and friendship   65
Create and cultivate our heart's salvation.

What germinated deep within us there,
What timid lips first stammered to themselves—
Failing at times, at times perhaps succeeding—
A moment's savage violence devours.   70
And only when it has matured for years
Does it at last appear in finished form.
What glitters is born for the moment alone;
What's genuine lives on for future generations.

Comic Actor. Don't talk to me of future generations.   75
Suppose I spoke of future generations,
Who'd entertain these people then?
They want some fun and they shall have it.
The presence of a decent actor
Should count for something too, I think.   80
If his delivery's smooth and pleasing,
The people's changing moods won't make him bitter;
In fact he likes a larger circle,
For then he's sure of his effect.
So just oblige me, write a model play!   85
Let Fantasy and her attendant choirs,

Reason, Understanding, Feeling, Passion,
Be heard! But please, take note, don't leave out Folly!

Director. But do make sure enough is happening!
    They come to watch and want to see some action.   90
    If lots of plots unwind before their eyes,
    So they can gawk dumbfounded,
    Then right away you'll win their praise,
    Gain widespread popularity.
    It's mass alone that moves the masses,   95
    For then each finds some bit that suits him.
    Who serves a lot, serves each guest something,
    And everyone leaves satisfied.
    If you present a piece, present it, please, in pieces!
    A stew like that will never let you down;   100
    It's easy to cook up and easy to dish out.
    And what's the use of serving something whole?
    Your audience is sure to pick it to pieces.

Poet.   You do not feel how worthless such a craft is!
    How little it befits a genuine artist!   105
    The fabrications of some fancy fellows
    Have, I see, become your standard.

Director. Your reproaches don't offend me:
    A man who wants to do a decent job
    Must first insist on proper tools.   110
    Remember, though, you're splitting softwood;
    Consider whom you're writing for!
    One person's driven here by boredom,
    Another comes here to digest a heavy dinner,
    And yet the very worst are those   115
    Who come from reading the daily papers.
    Flying on wings of curiosity,
    They rush here distracted, the way you'd go to carnival;
    The ladies display themselves in all their finery
    And put on a show that costs us nothing.   120
    What do you dream of there on your poetic heights?
    Why are you happy when a play's sold out?

Take one good look at our patrons!
Half are indifferent; half are simply crude.
One's hoping for a card game when the play gets out, 125
Another for a wild night at some wench's bosom.
Why do you poor fools plague the gentle muses so,
For such an end?
I tell you, keep producing—more, and more again—
Then you can never miss the mark. 130
Just try to keep your audience confused,
It's difficult to satisfy them . . .
But what's the matter? Ecstasy or agony?

Poet.   Go away and find some other lackey!
Do you expect a poet recklessly 135
To forfeit for your sake his human right,
The highest right that nature's granted him?
How does a poet move all hearts?
How does he conquer every element?
It's with the concord that wells from his breast 140
And draws the whole world back into his heart.
When nature spins indifferently and forces
The endless length of thread upon her spindle,
When the discordant multitude of beings
Clangs in disturbing dissonance, who measures off 145
That flowing, unrelenting sequence,
Brings it to life, so it beats rhythmically?
Who calls each thing to universal consecration,
That it may pulse in glorious accord?
Who lets the storm-wind work itself into a fury? 150
The red of twilight glow with solemn meaning?
Who scatters all the lovely flowers of spring
On paths where his beloved walks?
Who plaits the insignificant green leaves
Into a wreath that honors great achievements? 155
Who guards Olympus and assembles deities?
The power of man, revealed in poets.

Comic Actor. Well use them, then, those lovely powers,
And carry on with your poetic trade,

The way you'd carry on an amorous affair.   160
You meet by chance, feel something, stick around,
And bit by bit you find yourself entwined;
Your happiness increases, then it's threatened;
First you're in ecstasies, then agony approaches;
Before you know it, you've produced a novel.   165
Let's have a play that's like that too!
Just give us human life in its profusion!
Few will recognize it, though all live it,
And it's of interest anywhere you grab it.
Colorful images with little that is clear,   170
A lot of error, and a spark of truth—
That's how you brew the finest beer,
And everyone's refreshed and fortified.
The finest flower of youth will gather then
To hear your play and listen for the revelation;   175
Then every tender soul will suck
The milk of melancholy from your work;
Then you'll arouse now this, now that,
And each will see what lies within his heart.
The young are equally prepared to cry or laugh: 180
They worship lofty strains, rejoice in semblance;
Polished tastes are hard to please;
Developing minds are always grateful.

Poet.   Then give me back those days,
When I myself was still developing,   185
When springs of rushing songs
Continually poured forth,
When mists still veiled the world from me,
And every bud still promised wonders,
When I could pick a thousand flowers   190
That filled the valleys in abundance.
Then I had nothing, yet I had enough:
I yearned for truth, delighted in disguises.
Give me back those boundless drives,
The deep and painful joy,   195
The force of hatred, power of love—
Oh give me back my youth!

Comic Actor. Youth, my friend, is what you need,
    When enemies in battle press you,
    When some adorable girl is clinging   200
    Furiously about your neck,
    When in swift races distant wreaths
    Flash from a goal that's hard to reach,
    And when you drink away the night in revelry,
    After a wild and whirling dance.   205
    But to pluck the familiar strings of your lyre
    With courage and with grace,
    To wander, with gentle divagations,
    Toward a goal you've set yourself,
    That is the duty of old men—   210
    It doesn't diminish our respect for you.
    Age does not make us childish, as they say,
    But finds the true child that remains.

Director. You've bandied words enough,
    Now let me finally see some action!   215
    While you are turning compliments,
    Something useful could be happening.
    What good is it to talk of the right mood?
    It won't appear to him who hesitates.
    If you maintain that you are poets,   220
    Show some command of poetry.
    You know quite well what we require:
    We want to swallow potent drinks—
    Brew them without further delay!
    What doesn't get done today, will not get done tomorrow,   225
    And one should never waste a day.
    Let resolution seize what's possible
    Firmly by the hair,
    Then resolution won't let go
    And stays at work, because it has to.   230

    You know that in our German theaters
    You're free to try out what you want;
    So please, today, don't stint
    On backdrops and contraptions.

Use the greater and the lesser light of heaven,   235
Stars too—feel free to waste a few;
There is no shortage of fire and water,
Of rocky cliffs, of beasts and birds.
And thus within this narrow house of boards
The whole created sphere appears   240
And travels with judicious speed
From heaven through the world to hell.

Prologue in Heaven

> (The Lord. The Heavenly Hosts. Later Mephistopheles.
> The three Archangels come forward.)

Raphael. As of old the sun rings out
    To rival brother spheres in song
    And its appointed course fulfills,   245
    Thundering as it moves along.
    The sight of this gives angels strength,
    Although they cannot fathom it;
    The incomprehensibly high works
    Are glorious as on that first day.   250

Gabriel. Incomprehensible the speed
    With which earth's splendor spins around;
    The light of paradise takes turns
    With deep and dreadful night;
    In wide streams the ocean foams   255
    And churns against the deep cliff base,
    While cliff and sea are torn along
    In the eternal speed of the spheres' swift course.

Michael. The storm-winds roar in rivalry
    From sea to land, from land to sea,   260
    And form a furious chain
    Whose deep effects rage all around.
    There fiery devastation flashes,
    Lighting the thunderbolt's dark path,

And yet your envoys, Lord, revere 265
The gentle turning of your day.

All Three. The sight of this gives angels strength,
Because they cannot fathom you,
And all of your exalted works
Are glorious as on that first day. 270

Mephistopheles. Since you, O Lord, draw near once more
And ask us how things are these days,
And since you used to be quite glad to see me,
That's why I'm here among this servile crowd.
Excuse me, I can't use exalted words— 275
The present company may mock me,
But *you* would laugh if I declaimed with pathos—
If you had not renounced all laughter long ago.
I cannot sing of suns and universes;
I only see how humans plague themselves. 280
The small god of the world persists in his old ways—
He's as peculiar as on that first day.
Of course he'd fare a little better,
Had you not given him that gleam of heaven's light;
He calls it reason and employs it only 285
To be more bestial than a beast. He seems to me—
Your Grace must pardon the analogy—
Like one of those long-legged grasshoppers,
That always fly and flying spring
Into the grass and sing the same old song; 290
And if he'd only stayed there in the grass!
He pokes his nose in every sort of trash.

The Lord. Do you have nothing else to tell me?
Do you come constantly just to complain?
Are things on earth eternally not to your liking? 295

Mephistopheles. No, Lord! I find things there, as usual, pretty bad.
I pity humans in the misery of their days—
Don't even like to plague the poor things anymore.

The Lord. Do you know Faust?

Mephistopheles.   The doctor?

The Lord.   My servant!

Mephistopheles. Truly! He serves you in a singular way.   300
     That fool despises earthly food and drink.
     Some ferment drives him far away;
     He is half conscious of his madness.
     From heaven he demands the brightest stars
     And from the earth the highest pleasures,   305
     And nothing near and nothing far
     Can satisfy his heaving breast.

The Lord. Although he serves me in confusion now,
     I shall soon lead him into clarity.
     For when a sapling sprouts, the gardener knows   310
     That flowers and fruit will grace the coming years.

Mephistopheles. What will you wager? You will lose him yet,
     If you'll grant me permission
     To lead him gently down my alley!

The Lord. As long as he lives on the earth,   315
     That long it's not forbidden you.
     Humans will err as long as they strive.

Mephistopheles. I thank you, for I've never really cared
     To deal with the dead.
     What I like best are round and rosy cheeks.   320
     When a corpse comes calling I am not at home;
     Like a cat I like my mice alive.

The Lord. Well, then, it's up to you!
     Draw his spirit from its source,
     And if you can possess him, lead him   325

Down along your path,
And stand ashamed, when you have to confess
That a good man, in his dark yearning,
Still knows the right path well.

Mephistopheles. That's fine! It won't take long.   330
I'm not concerned about my wager.
If I succeed, you must allow me
To proclaim my triumph loudly.
Dust shall he eat,[3] and with an appetite,
Just like my relative, the famous serpent.   335

The Lord. There too you're free to do just what you please,
For I have never hated those like you.
Of all the spirits that negate,
The rogue who scoffs concerns me least.
Human activity too easily grows slack;   340
Man's all too fond of unconditional rest;
And so I'm glad to give him a companion,
Who tempts, works, and creates—in devilish fashion.
But you, true sons of God,
Rejoice in this abundant, living beauty!   345
Let all that comes to be, and works and lives eternally,
Enfold you in the gentle bonds of love;
And what appears and floats and fluctuates,
Make steadfast with enduring thoughts.

(Heaven closes, the Archangels disperse.)

Mephistopheles (alone). I like to see the old man now and then,   350
And take good care not to fall foul of him.
It's quite genteel of such a noble lord
To address the very devil in such human terms.

---

3. Cf. Genesis 3:14.

Part I of the Tragedy

Night

(Faust sits restlessly at his desk, in a
high-vaulted, narrow Gothic room.)

Faust.   Now I've studied philosophy,
        Jurisprudence too, and medicine,   355
        And even, sad to say, theology,
        Thoroughly, with great exertion.
        And here I am, poor fool,
        Not one bit wiser than before!
        Oh yes, I'm called a master, doctor in fact,   360
        And for ten years or so I've dragged—
        Up and down, and every which way—
        My students around by the nose,
        And see that we can't know a thing!
        It burns my very heart away.   365
        I'm cleverer than those idiots, yes,
        Those doctors, masters, scribes, and priests;
        No doubts or scruples trouble me,
        I'm not afraid of Hell or devil—
        But in return I'm robbed of every joy;   370
        I don't pretend to know a thing that matters;
        I don't pretend that I could teach a thing
        That would make people better or transform them.
        I've neither property nor wealth,
        Nor any worldly honor and glory;   375
        A dog couldn't stand to live like this!
        So I've devoted myself to magic,
        To see if through some spirit's power and voice
        I may not learn things that are hidden;
        So I'll no longer have to declaim   380
        With sweating brow, what I don't know;
        So I'll perceive what holds the world
        Together in its inmost core,
        See all potencies and seeds,
        And traffic in words no more.   385

        Oh would that for the final time,
        Full moon, you looked down on my anguish,

You for whom I've watched and waited
Many a midnight, at this desk.
Above my books and papers then,   390
O melancholy friend, you would appear!
Oh how I wish that I might wander
On mountain heights in your dear light,
Might float through mountain caves with spirits,
Might weave across the dusky meadows,   395
And bathing in your dew, recover,
Relieved of all my hazy knowledge!

Am I still stuck inside this prison?
Infernal, dreary hole in the wall,
Where even heaven's precious light   400
Breaks dimly through the colored panes!
Constricted by high stacks of books,
Which worms have gnawed and dust has buried,
Which pile up to the vaulted ceiling,
With smoke-stained papers stuffed between them; 405
This hole beset with jars and bottles,
Crammed full of instruments
And every sort of antique apparatus—
That's your world! You call that a world!

Do you still wonder why your heart   410
Contracts so anxiously within your breast?
Why inexplicable pains
Obstruct your vital forces?
Instead of living nature,
Which God created man to dwell in,   415
Assorted bones and skeletons
Surround you here—and soot and rot.

Flee! Out to open countryside!
Will not this book of mysteries,
Penned by Nostradamus' hand,[4]   420

4.   Michel de Notredame was a sixteenth-century physician and astrologer who published a book of prophecies.

Provide you with sufficient guidance?
You'll learn the course of every star,
And then, when nature is your teacher,
That power of soul will be unlocked
Which lets one spirit talk to others.   425
In vain your dry deliberation here
Tries to explain the sacred signs:
You're floating close beside me, spirits;
Answer me, if you can hear me!
    (*He opens the book and sees the sign of the macrocosm.*)
What sudden rapture streams   430
Through all my senses at this sight!
I feel life's youthful, holy joy,
New-glowing, running through my nerves and veins.
Was it some god who drew these signs
That quiet all my inner turmoil,   435
Fill my poor heart with happiness,
And now by some mysterious impulse
Disclose the powers of nature all around me?
Am I a god? I sense such light!
In these clear lines I see   440
Ever active nature unveiled to me.
At last I understand the wise man's words:
"The world of spirits is not closed,
Your senses are; your heart is dead!
Arise, young man, and bathe undaunted   445
Your earthly breast in dawn's first red!"
    (*He looks at the sign.*)
How all things weave into a whole,
Each works and lives within the other!
Heavenly powers ascending and descending
Pass golden pails to one another!   450
Swinging on wings fragrant with blessings,
From heaven they spread throughout the earth,
And all ring out in concert through the all!

What a spectacle! Alas, merely a spectacle!
Where shall I grasp you, infinite nature?   455
Where, you breasts? You sources of all life,
On which both heaven and earth depend,

To which my withered breast would cling;
You flow and nourish—must I thirst in vain?
  (*Indignantly he turns the page and sees
  the sign of the Earth Spirit.*)
How differently this sign affects me!   460
You, Spirit of the Earth, are closer to me:
Now I feel my powers heightened;
Now I'm glowing with new wine;
I feel the courage to go out into the world,
To bear earth's grief and joy,   465
To battle with its tempests,
And not to tremble in the crashing shipwreck.
The clouds are gathering above me—
The moon conceals its light—
The lamp is going out!   470
It's misty now—and red rays flicker
Around my head—a shudder
Drifts down from the vaulted ceiling—
Comes over me!
I feel you floating round me, Spirit I invoked.   475
Show yourself!
Ah, how my heart is torn!
And all my senses stirred
To strange new feelings!
I feel my heart surrender utterly to you!   480
You must! You must! If it costs my life!

  (*He grasps the book and mysteriously pronounces
  the sign of the Spirit. A reddish flame flickers
  and the Spirit appears in the flame.*)

Spirit. Who summons me?

Faust (*turning away*).   Dreadful sight!

Spirit. With mighty powers you've drawn me to you,
You've long sucked at my sphere,
And now—

Faust.   Alas, I can't endure you!   485

Spirit.   Breathlessly you begged to see me,
            To hear my voice, to look upon my face;
            Your potent supplications moved me—
            And here I am! But what pathetic terror
            Has overcome the superman! Where is the clamoring soul,   490
            The breast that once created a world within itself
            And housed and carried it, the breast that swelled
            With trembling joy, aspiring to our spirit realm?
            Where is that Faust whose voice rang out, that Faust
            Who thrust himself on me with all his might?   495
            Is it you? You who shiver to the depths,
            When my least breath blows on you?
            A frightened, wriggling worm?

Faust.   Fiery figure, shall I yield to you?
            It's me; I'm Faust, your equal!   500

Spirit.   In surging tides of life, in storms of action,
            Up and down I well,
            Back and forth I weave!
            Birth and grave,
            An eternal sea,   505
            A shifting fabric,
            A glowing life—
            I toil at the whirring loom of time
            And make the living garment of God.

Faust.   You range the world, industrious spirit,   510
            How close to you I feel!

Spirit.   You're equal to the spirit you can comprehend,
            Not to me!
                (Disappears.)

Faust (collapsing). Not to you?
            To whom then?   515
            I, God's very image!
            Not even to you! (He hears knocking.)

Death! I know that sound—it's my assistant—
My loveliest happiness destroyed!
Oh why must that pedantic bore   520
Disrupt these all-embracing visions!

> (*Wagner in his nightshirt and nightcap, holding
> a lamp in his hand. Faust turns reluctantly.*)

Wagner. Excuse me! I heard you declaiming—
From some Greek tragedy, no doubt?
Now there's an art from which I'd profit:
It's most effective nowadays.   525
I've often heard it recommended;
They say an actor could instruct a priest.

Faust. Yes, if the priest's a comic actor,
As does occur from time to time.

Wagner. Alas! When one is shut inside one's study   530
And rarely gets out, even on a holiday,
And sees the world from far away, as through a telescope,
How can one guide men with one's rhetoric?

Faust. Unless you feel it, you will never hunt it down,
Unless it comes from your own soul,   535
Compelling every heart that hears it
With primal power that satisfies.
But you just sit there cutting and pasting,
Concocting a stew from other people's scraps,
And fanning some paltry flames   540
From your little pile of embers!
Children and monkeys will admire you,
If that's to your taste—
But you will never touch men's hearts,
Unless your own heart's speaking.   545

Wagner. An orator's success depends on his delivery;
In this I feel I'm far behind.

Faust.   Earn your living honestly!
          Don't be a fool with jingling bells!
          Understanding and good sense   550
          Present themselves without much art;
          And if you really have something to say,
          What need is there to hunt for words?
          Those oratorical displays, in which you crimp
          Bits of tinsel for mankind,   555
          Are as refreshing as the foggy wind
          That rustles through dry autumn leaves!

Wagner.   God help me! Art is long,
          And life is short.[5]
          How often, in my critical endeavors,   560
          My mind and heart are filled with doubt.
          How hard it is to acquire the skills
          By means of which one can ascend to primary sources!
          And well before one's halfway there,
          One's bound to die, poor devil.   565

Faust.   Is parchment, then, the sacred well
          Whose waters will forever quench your thirst?
          You'll never find refreshment,
          Unless it wells from your own soul.

Wagner.   Excuse me! But it's such a great delight   570
          To enter into the spirit of each age,
          To ascertain how wise men long before us thought
          And how in recent times we've made such glorious progress.

Faust.   Oh yes, such progress—to the very stars!
          My friend, for us the ages of the past   575
          Are as a book with seven seals.
          And what you call the spirit of the ages—
          Why, in the end it's simply your own spirit,

---

5.   An example of one of the "scraps" Faust has just mentioned (539). Wagner is quoting
the Latin author Seneca, who is himself quoting the Greek physician Hippocrates.

In which the ages are reflected.
And what a sorry picture that can be! 580
Enough to make you flee at first sight:
A pile of trash, an attic full of junk,
At best a tragedy of crowns and kingdoms
That's full of grand, sententious sayings
To suit the mouthing puppets in a play! 585

Wagner. But the world! The human heart and mind!
Everyone would like to know a bit about them.

Faust. Yes, what you call knowing!
For who can call the child by its true name?
The few who've known a bit about it, 590
And foolishly refused to hide their brimming hearts,
Revealing their feelings and their visions to the rabble,
Have always been the ones we crucify and burn.
Now please, my friend, it's late at night,
We need to call it quits for now. 595

Wagner. I would have liked to stay awake forever,
Engaging in these learned conversations.
But let me ask you one or two more questions
Tomorrow, since that's Easter Sunday.
I've been a conscientious student 600
And know a lot—it's true—but want to know it all.
(*Exit.*)

Faust (alone). How can a head that obstinately clings
To shallow things not lose all hope?
With greedy hands it digs for treasures—
Rejoices when it finds a worm or two! 605

How dare a human voice like that
Speak here, where spirits filled the air?
And yet! This once I thank you,
Though you're the poorest of the sons of earth.
You tore me free from the despair 610
That almost made me lose my senses.

That apparition loomed so high above me,
I felt quite dwarflike in comparison.

I, God's own image, who already thought
Myself quite near the mirror of eternal truth,   615
I, who partook of heaven's dazzling clarity
And had cast off my earthly husk,
I, more than cherub, whose unfettered powers
Presciently presumed to flow through nature's veins
And to enjoy, creatively, the life of gods,   620
How have I had to expiate this trespass!
A thunder-word has dashed me to the ground.

I can't presume to claim that I'm your equal!
Though I possessed the power to draw you,
I had no power at all to keep you here.   625
In that ecstatic moment,
I felt so small and yet so great;
But brutally you thrust me back,
Down into man's uncertain lot.
Then who will teach me? What must I avoid?   630
And am I to obey this urge?
Alas, our very deeds, as well as what we suffer,
Impede the courses of our lives.

And foreign matter weighs us down,
Encumbering what's most glorious in the human spirit;   635
When we attain to this world's goods,
We call what's better mere illusion.
The glorious feelings that once gave us life
Grow rigid in the earthly turmoil.

Though once imagination spread bold wings   640
Expectantly toward eternity,
It's now content with little room,
As joy after joy is shattered in time's whirlpool.
Soon care nests deep inside your heart,
And there it works its secret sorrows;   645
Uneasily it rocks, disturbing rest and pleasure;

Relentlessly it hides behind new masks,
Appears as house and yard, as wife and child,
As fire, as water, dagger, poison;
You quake at things that never happen   650
And weep continually for what you have not lost.

Not like the gods! I feel it all too deeply;
I'm like a worm that tunnels through the dust,
And as it feeds and lives in dust is crushed
And buried by some passing traveler's step.   655

Is it not dust, all this that fills these hundred pigeonholes
And makes the high walls seem so narrow?
The rubbish and the endless trappings
That weigh upon me in this moth-world?
Is this where I'm to find what's lacking?   660
Am I perhaps to read in countless books,
That people everywhere endure such torture,
That here and there there's been a happy man?
Why do you leer at me, you hollow skull,
Unless your brain like mine once in confusion   665
Sought the light day, but in the heavy twilight,
Yearning for truth, went woefully astray?
And how you mock me, instruments,
With your wheels and brushes, cylinders and clamps;[6]
I stood before the gate; you were to be my keys,   670
Yet your elaborate bits won't lift the latch.[7]
In vain we tear at nature's veil:
She's full of secrets in broad daylight,
And what she won't reveal to you,
You'll never wrench from her with screws and levers.   675
Old apparatus that I never used,
You're here because my father needed you.
Old parchment, you grow grey with soot,

---

6.   The "wheels and brushes" may refer to the parts of an electrostatic generator. The first such instrument was constructed in 1663 by Otto von Guericke (long after the time of the historical Faust).

7.   The "bit" is the part of a key that engages with the lock-lever.

While this dim, smoky lamp burns at my desk.
Far better to have squandered what I own,   680
Than sit here sweating, burdened by its weight.
What your fathers have bequeathed you,
Earn it, in order to make it your own.
What we don't use becomes a heavy burden;
The moment can only use what it creates.   685

Why does that spot attract my gaze?
Is that small flask a magnet to my eyes?
And what sweet brightness suddenly surrounds me,
Like moonlight drifting round us in nocturnal woods?
Inimitable vial, I greet you,   690
With reverence I lift you down!
In you I honor human ingenuity and art.
Distillate of every gentle sleeping potion,
Quintessence of all fine and deadly powers,
Do your master one last favor!   695
I look on you—at once my pain subsides;
I hold you and my striving moderates;
The flood-tide of my spirit ebbs away.
You guide me out toward the open sea;
Reflecting waters sparkle at my feet—   700
A new day lures me to new shores.

Swaying lightly, a chariot of fire,
Swings toward me! I feel prepared
To penetrate the ether on new paths,
Toward new spheres of pure activity.   705
This exalted life, this divine rapture—
How can you, a worm just now, deserve it?
Yes, turn your back decisively
Upon the gentle earthly sun!
Presume to tear apart the portals   710
That every man tries to creep past unseen.
Now is the time to demonstrate by deeds,
That human dignity won't yield to the high gods,
Time not to quake at that dark hollow
In which imagination damns itself to tortures,   715

Time to strive toward that passageway
Around whose narrow mouth all hell flames forth,
And to resolve serenely on this step,
Even at the risk of utter dissolution.

So come then, purest crystal goblet!   720
Come out now from your ancient case;
I have not thought of you for many years!
You used to sparkle at ancestral feasts,
You used to cheer the solemn guests,
As toasts were pledged by one man to the next.   725
Each drinker had to explicate in verse
The elaborate engravings that adorn you,
Then drain your hollow bowl in just one draft.
These things remind me of those nights when I was young;
But now I'll hand you to no neighbor,   730
I'll show no genius for interpretation;
This is a juice that intoxicates quickly,
Filling your hollow skull with its brown flood.
I prepared it and I choose it:
With all my soul I pledge this final drink   735
In solemn festal greeting to the rising day!
    (*He puts the goblet to his lips.*)

    (*Bells and choral song.*)

Choir of Angels. Christ is risen!
        Joy to the mortal,
        Around whom the fatal,
        Subtle, ancestral   740
        Failings once wound.

Faust. What's that low tone, what's this bright sound
        That pulls the glass so violently from my mouth?
        Can you dull bells already be announcing
        The first triumphant hour of Easter day?   745
        You choirs already singing those consoling verses
        That, in the tomb's dark night, rang out from angel lips,
        Assuring us of a new covenant?

Choir of Women. With fragrant ointments
         We had tended him,   750
         We, his faithful ones,
         Had laid him down;
         Wound clean linen
         Cloths around him,
         Alas, and we find   755
         Christ no longer here.

Choir of Angels. Christ is risen!
         Blest is the loving one,
         Who has now passed
         The grievous, but healing   760
         And strengthening test.

Faust.   You sounds of heaven, powerful and gentle,
         Why do you seek me in the dust?
         Ring out where there are more receptive souls.
         I hear your tidings well enough, but don't have faith,   765
         And miracles are faith's beloved children.
         I dare not strive toward the spheres
         Where those sweet tidings sound;
         And yet these tones, familiar from my youth,
         Now call me back to life as well.   770
         It used to be that heaven's loving kiss would fall
         On me, there in the solemn Sabbath stillness;
         The bell's full tone seemed filled with prescient meaning,
         And ardent prayer was my delight.
         A sweet incomprehensible desire   775
         Would drive me out into the fields and woods,
         And shedding countless tears,
         I'd feel a new world come to be.
         This very hymn announced the happy games of youth,
         The unfettered joy of spring festivities.   780
         And now, with childlike feelings, memory
         Holds me back from that last solemn step.
         Sound on, sweet songs of heaven!
         A tear wells up and I belong to earth once more!

Choir of Disciples. If then the buried one, 785
    Sublime while he lived,
    Now in his glory
    Is risen above,
    In ecstatic becoming
    Draws near creative bliss, 790
    Alas! At earth's breast,
    We're here to grieve.
    Can he have left his own
    Thirsting down here?
    Alas, we weep 795
    At your happiness, master!

Choir of Angels. Christ is risen
    From the womb of perdition;
    Blissfully tear yourselves
    Free from your bonds! 800
    You who actively praise him,
    In manifest love,
    Feeding each hungry one,
    Preaching to everyone,
    Promising blessedness, 805
    The Master is near to you,
    Yes, he is here for you!

Outside the Gate

(All sorts of people setting out on walks.)

Some Apprentices. But why that way?

Others. We're going out to the hunting lodge.

The First Group. We'd rather walk down to the mill. 810

One Apprentice. You ought to try the inn on the river.

Second Apprentice. The path there's not the least bit pretty.

Second Group. And what about you?

Third Apprentice.　　　　　　　　I'm going with the others.

Fourth Apprentice. Come up to Burgdorf—there you'll find
　　　The prettiest girls, the best beer too,　　　　　　　815
　　　And first-rate fights besides.

Fifth Apprentice. But why so eager—
　　　Is your hide itching for another blow?
　　　I won't go there; that place fills me with dread.

Servant Girl. No, no! I'm going back to town.　　　　820

Second Girl. He's sure to be down by those poplars.

First Girl. That won't do me much good;
　　　It's you he'll walk beside,
　　　And you're the one he'll dance with.
　　　What good's your happiness to me?　　　　　　825

Second Girl. I'm sure he's not alone today,
　　　He said he'd bring his friend, the one with curly hair.

Student. Just look at the way those wenches walk!
　　　Come on! We'll stroll along beside them;
　　　Stout beer and strong tobacco,　　　　　　　830
　　　A girl in a fancy dress—that's to my taste.

Young Lady. Just take a peek at those good-looking boys!
　　　Isn't it an awful shame,
　　　When they could have some first-class company,
　　　That they run after such low game!　　　　　835

Second Student (to the first). Not so fast! There come two more;
  They're dressed adorably,
  And one of them's my neighbor;
  I've got a soft spot for that girl.
  They're walking so demurely,   840
  But in the end they'll let us join them.

First Student. Forget it! I don't like to feel inhibited.
  Come quickly, or we'll lose our prey.
  The hand that holds a broom on Saturday,
  Is the one that caresses most gently on Sunday.   845

Citizen. No, I can't say I care for our new mayor!
  Now he's in office, he gets bolder by the day,
  And what's he doing for this town?
  Don't things get worse and worse each day?
  More regulations to obey   850
  And higher taxes than before.

Beggar (singing). Good gentlemen and pretty ladies,
  With your fine clothes and rosy cheeks,
  Please turn this way and look at me
  And see and help me in my need!   855
  Don't let me grind my tune in vain,
  How happy is the generous man!
  And on this day all celebrate
  Please let me reap abundantly.

Another Citizen. There's nothing better on a holiday,   860
  Than talk of war and rumors of battle,
  When far away, in distant Turkey,
  The armies pummel one another.
  You stand at the window, drain your glass,
  And watch bright ships glide down the river;   865
  Then you stroll home at night a happy man,
  Extolling peace and peaceful times.

Third Citizen. Yes, neighbor, that's what I like too,
> Why, let them split their heads apart,
> And let the whole world fall to pieces,   870
> As long as nothing changes here at home.

Old Woman (to the young ladies). My, my, how fine! Such fresh young
> beauties!
> Who could resist the urge to stare at you?
> Don't be so haughty! I'll be quiet!
> Of course, I could procure the things you're wishing for— 875

Young Lady. Come, Agatha! I'm very careful
> Not to be seen in public with such witches;
> Though on St. Andrew's Eve she let
> Me see my future lover in the flesh—

Second Young Lady. She showed me mine in her crystal ball,   880
> A soldier, with his dashing friends;
> I've sought him here, I've sought him there,
> But never seem to find him.

Soldiers. Castles with high
> Ramparts and battlements,   885
> Girls with disdainful
> Thoughts and proud sentiments,
> These let me conquer!
> Bold the endeavor,
> Glorious the spoils!   890

> Let the loud trumpet
> Announce our advances;
> Whether toward pleasure,
> Or to destruction,
> Onwards we storm!   895
> This is the life!
> Castles and maidens
> Have to surrender.
> Bold the endeavor,

Glorious the spoils!   900
And the soldiers
Go marching on.

(Enter Faust and Wagner.)

Faust. The streams and brooks are freed of ice
By the gentle, quickening gaze of spring;
Expectant joy turns valleys green;   905
The winter, old now and infirm,
Withdraws to craggy mountain tops.
From there it volleys, as it flees,
Impotent showers of icy grain
In stripes across the verdant fields;   910
The sun can tolerate nothing white:
All things begin to develop and strive;
The sun would quicken the earth with color:
Although the landscape still lacks flowers,
It blooms with people dressed for Easter.   915
Then turn, so you are looking back
From these heights toward the city.
Out of the dark and hollow gate
A colorful crowd is bursting forth.
All are enjoying the sun today.   920
They celebrate the Lord's resurrection,
For they themselves are risen today:
Out of dreary rooms in low, squat houses,
Out of bonds of work and business,
Out of oppressive roofs and gables,   925
Out of tight, constricting alleys,
Out of the solemn night of churches,
They've all been brought to light today.
Look! See how quickly the multitude
Disperses through the gardens and meadows;   930
See how the river, far and wide,
Is rocking countless pleasure boats;
Overloaded to the point of sinking,
A last boat pulls out from the shore.
Even from distant trails on the mountain,   935
Colorful clothes are blinking at us.
And now I hear the noise of the village;

This truly is the people's heaven,
Where, satisfied, each one exults:
Here at last I'm fully human!   940

Wagner.   Doctor, to walk with you like this
Is an honor from which I profit greatly.
And yet, I wouldn't want to be alone here,
For I'm averse to all that's coarse.
Fiddling, shouting—bowling too—   945
I really hate that sort of racket;
They romp as if an evil spirit drove them,
And call it joy, and call it song.

Peasants (dancing and singing under the linden tree).
A shepherd dressed up for the dance;
In jacket bright, with wreath and bands,   950
He decked himself out fine.
Down by the linden tree he found
A great crowd spinning wildly round.
Hey ho! Hey ho!
Hip hey, hip ho, hey ho!   955
So went the fiddle-bow.

He squeezed himself into the throng,
A pretty maiden whirled along,
He jabbed her with his elbow;
The fresh girl turned around and said,   960
"Have you no brains inside your head?"
Hey ho! Hey ho!
Hip hey, hip ho, hey ho!
Don't be so rude, young fellow!

But rapidly they reeled about,   965
Turned to the left, turned to the right,
My, how the skirts were flying.
They grew quite red, they grew quite warm,
They rested, panting, arm in arm.
Hey ho! Hey ho!   970

Hip hey, hip ho, hey ho!
A hip beside an elbow.

"Oh please, don't be quite so familiar!
For many a man has proved untrue
To the girl he calls his bride!"   975
And yet he coaxed her to the side,
While from the linden tree rang wide:
Hey ho! Hey ho!
Hip hey, hip ho, hey ho!
Shouts and a fiddle-bow.   980

Old Peasant. Why, Doctor, it's so kind of you
　　　　To join us on our holiday,
　　　　And, learned as you are, to walk
　　　　Among this throng of common folk.
　　　　Accept our finest tankard, please,   985
　　　　We've filled it with fresh drink for you;
　　　　I raise it to you with the wish
　　　　That it not only quench your thirst,
　　　　But that each drop it holds will add
　　　　To the number of your days.   990

Faust.　For this refreshing drink I thank you,
　　　　And in return I wish you health as well.

　　　　(The people gather in a circle around Faust.)

Old Peasant. Really, sir, it's good of you,
　　　　To come out on this happy day;
　　　　For long ago, when times were bad,   995
　　　　You were the one who helped us out!
　　　　Many of us are alive today,
　　　　Because your father tore us
　　　　From the clutches of a raging fever
　　　　And stopped the plague right in its tracks.   1000
　　　　You too, a young man at that time,
　　　　Went into every hospital;
　　　　Many a corpse they carried forth,
　　　　But in good health you'd come back out;

| | You weathered many harsh ordeals; | 1005 |
| | A greater Helper helped our helper. | |

All. A health to this deserving man,
       That he may help for years to come!

Faust. Then bow your heads to the Helper on high,
         Who teaches us to help and sends his aid.   1010

          (He continues on his way with Wagner.)

Wagner. What a feeling the reverence of this multitude
          Must arouse in you, great man!
          Happy is he who can derive
          Such profit from his talents!
          Fathers point you out to their sons,   1015
          They all ask questions, throng, rush toward you;
          The fiddle stops, the dancers pause,
          You walk past and they stand in rows,
          Their caps go flying in the air;
          They almost fall on bended knees,   1020
          As if the sacrament were passing by.

Faust. It's just a few more steps up to that stone,
         We'll take a rest here from our walk.
         Here, lost in thought, I often sat alone,
         Tormenting myself with prayer and fasting.   1025
         So full of hope, so firm in faith,
         By weeping, sighing, wringing my hands,
         I thought I'd wrest the end of that affliction
         From the Lord of heaven. But now
         The multitude's applause rings out like mockery.   1030
         If you could only look inside my heart and see
         How little father and son
         Deserve this reputation!
         My father was an undistinguished gentleman,
         Who pondered nature and its sacred cycles   1035
         With honest effort, though in his own
         Idiosyncratic ways;
         In the company of the initiate,

He locked himself inside black kitchens
Where, following endless recipes, he poured   1040
Inimical ingredients together.
There, in a tepid bath the bold red lion,[8]
A fearless suitor, had to wed the lily.
Over an open flame, the two
Were forced into a second bridal chamber.   1045
Then in bright colors the young queen
Appeared inside the flask.
Here was the medicine, the patients died,
And who got better? No one asked.
So we, with diabolical electuaries,   1050
Stormed through these hills and valleys
And caused more damage than the plague.
To thousands I administered that poison;
They wasted away, and now I have to listen
As people praise the ruthless murderers.   1055

Wagner. Why let that trouble you?
           Doesn't a decent man do well enough,
           If he practices the art transmitted to him,
           Conscientiously and accurately?
           If you respect your father when you're young,   1060
           Then you'll be glad to learn from him;
           If, as an adult, you advance the science,
           Your son can reach a higher goal.

Faust.   How happy is he who can still hope
           To surface from this sea of error!   1065
           We do not know the very thing we need to,
           And what we know is of no use.
           But do not let us spoil the beauty of this hour
           With melancholy thoughts.
           See how the huts, against the green surround,   1070
           Shimmer in the glowing evening sun.

8. The "red lion" is probably red mercuric oxide; the "lily" is probably hydrochloric acid.
The "young queen," which is supposed to result from their union, is the philosopher's stone,
said to be capable of turning base metals into gold, as well as being reputed to be an elixir
of life.

The day's outlived, the sun recedes and fades;
It hurries on and fosters new life elsewhere.
Oh for a pair of wings to lift me from the ground,
That I might strive to follow it forever! 1075
Then in eternal evening rays I'd see
The quiet world down at my feet,
Each peak ablaze, the valleys all at rest,
And brooks of silver flowing into golden rivers.
Then the wild mountain with its chasms 1080
Would not impede my godlike course—
Already the ocean with its sun-warmed bays
Begins to spread out under my astonished eyes.
At last the goddess seems to sink away;
And yet a new urge now awakens; 1085
I hurry on, to drink her everlasting light,
Before me day, behind me night,
The sky above me, and the waves below.
A lovely dream, although she's disappearing.
Alas! my body can extend no wings 1090
To accompany my spirit's flight.
And yet we're all born with a feeling
That strains to rise and presses onward,
When lost in blue space high above us,
A skylark trills its piercing song; 1095
When over high, spruce-covered bluffs
An eagle floats on outstretched wings,
And over lowlands, over lakes,
The cranes are striving homeward.

Wagner. I've often had strange notions too, 1100
　　　　But I have never felt an urge like that.
　　　　One's eyes soon tire of woods and fields;
　　　　I'll never envy the bird its pinions.
　　　　How different are those mental pleasures
　　　　That carry us from book to book, from page to page! 1105
　　　　Then winter nights grow mild and fair,
　　　　A blessed life warms all your limbs,
　　　　And oh! When you unroll some precious parchment,
　　　　Does not the whole of heaven descend on you?

Faust.   You're conscious only of one drive;   1110
            Oh never learn to know the other!
            For two souls dwell, alas, within my breast,
            And one would tear itself away and leave the other;
            One clings, with clasping limbs,
            To the world in earthy love-delight;   1115
            The other, rising fiercely from the dust,
            Soars up to high ancestral regions.
            If there are spirits weaving through the air,
            Who rule the realm between the earth and heaven,
            Descend now from your golden mists,   1120
            And lead me to a new life filled with color!
            If only I possessed a magic cape,
            To carry me to foreign lands!
            I would not trade it for the richest garments,
            No, not for the robes of a king.   1125

Wagner.   Don't summon the demonic horde
            That streams and spreads out through the atmosphere,
            Preparing multifarious dangers,
            From all directions, for the human race.
            From the north their sharp and ghostly teeth   1130
            Bite into you, their tongues like pointed arrows;
            From the east they come and parch you,
            And feed upon the moisture in your lungs.
            And while from desert sands the equator sends
            Winds that heap their glowing embers on your brow,   1135
            The west brings swarms that first refresh,
            Then inundate you and the fields and meadows.
            They're glad to listen, delighted to harm,
            Glad to obey, since they love to deceive us,
            Act as if they're heaven-sent,   1140
            Whisper angelically, although they're lying.
            But come, let's go! The world's turned grey,
            The air's grown cool, the fog is settling in.
            At night one learns to value one's own home.
            Why do you stand like that and stare in wonder?   1145
            In that grey dusk what can exert such hold on you?

Faust.   That black dog running through the grain and stubble.

Wagner. I noticed him before; he didn't seem important.

Faust.   Look carefully! What do you think he is?

Wagner. I'd say he was a poodle, doggedly bent   1150
            On sniffing out his master's traces.

Faust.   Have you observed him hunting in wide spirals
            Around us, slowly circling closer in?
            And if I'm not mistaken, a whirl of fire
            Trails along the path behind him.   1155

Wagner. Perhaps that is an optical illusion;
            A black poodle is all I see.

Faust.   It seems to me he's drawing subtle, magic loops
            Around our feet, to bind us in the future.

Wagner. I see him jumping anxiously around us,   1160
            Because he sees two strangers, not his master.

Faust.   The circle's getting tight, he's very near us!

Wagner. You see! This is a dog and not a ghost.
            He growls and is suspicious, crouches on his haunches.
            He wags his tail. All in good canine fashion.   1165

Faust.   Come and join us! Come here!

Wagner. He's just a silly poodle.
            Stand still and he'll wait patiently,
            Or call him and he'll strive to climb on you;
            If you lose something, he'll go fetch it;   1170
            He'll jump in the water when you throw a stick.

Faust.   You're right, I find no trace
          Of spirit; it's just training.

Wagner. Even a wise man's fond of a well-trained dog.
          This one especially merits your goodwill,   1175
          For he's a first-class scholar,
          Whom your own students educated.

          (They pass through the city gate.)

Study

Faust (entering with the poodle).
          I have abandoned fields and meadows,
          Which night now blankets in thick darkness,
          Rousing the better soul inside us   1180
          With prescient and holy dread.
          Wild longings now are lulled to sleep
          And with them all tempestuous action;
          The love of humankind awakens,
          Awakened is the love of God.   1185

          Be quiet, poodle! Stop running back and forth!
          Why are you snuffling around at the doorway?
          Go lie down there behind the stove,
          And I'll give you my finest pillow.
          Out on the mountain path your scampering   1190
          And springing entertained us, yes,
          But now accept my hospitality,
          And be a welcome, quiet guest.

          When here inside our narrow cell,
          The friendly lamp's ablaze once more,   1195
          Then all grows bright inside us too,
          Inside the heart that knows itself.
          Reason begins to speak again,
          And hope once more begins to bloom;

We long for living waters then,   1200
Oh, for the very fount of life.

Stop growling, poodle! Your beastly noise
Is not in tune with the sacred sounds
That now envelop my entire soul.
We're used to the fact that people mock   1205
Whatever they don't understand
And grumble at the good and beautiful,
Because it's far too onerous—
Can a dog want to growl at it too?

No longer, though, despite my best intentions,   1210
Does satisfaction well within my breast,
Why must the stream run dry so soon
And leave us lying here to thirst?
I've all too much experience of this.
But still, this want can be supplied: 1215
We learn to value heavenly things;
We long for revelation,
And nowhere does that burn with greater splendor,
Than here in the New Testament.
I feel compelled to turn to the primary source, 1220
And to translate
This sacred text from the original
Faithfully into my beloved German.

   (He opens a volume and gets ready to write.)

It is written, "In the beginning was the *Word*!"
I'm stuck already! How can I continue?   1225
I can't place such great value on the *Word*;
I'll have to render it some other way,
If I'm illumined by the Spirit.
It is written, "In the beginning was the *Mind*."
But contemplate this first line well;   1230
Don't let your pen be overhasty!
Is it *Mind* that makes and does all things?
It should say, "In the beginning was the *Power*!"
Yet, even as I write this down,

Something tells me I won't stick with it.   1235
The Spirit's helping me! Suddenly I see,
And comforted I write, "In the beginning was the *Deed*!"

If I'm to share this room with you,
Then, poodle, stop that howling,
Stop that barking!   1240
I can't stand having
Such disturbing company in here.
One of us
Must vacate this cell.
I'm sorry to rescind my invitation;   1245
The door is open, you are free to go.
But what do I see now!
Can this be happening naturally?
Is this an apparition? Or reality?
My poodle's growing long and wide!   1250
He's standing up aggressively—
This isn't the form of a dog!
What phantom have I brought into the house!
He looks just like a hippopotamus,
With fiery eyes and terrifying jaws.   1255
Yes, now I've got you!
On such half-breeds from hell,
The Key of Solomon works well.[9]

Spirits (in the passage).
One of ours is caught inside!
Do not follow him, stay out here!   1260
Like a fox in a snare,
One of hell's lynxes is trapped in there.
Cautiously then!
Glide up, glide down,
Backwards, forwards,   1265
Soon he'll escape the bonds that hold him.
Help him if you can,

---

9. The *clavicula salomonis* or "Key of Solomon" is a handbook of magic that purports to go back to the time of the Old Testament King Solomon.

Do not forsake him,
For he has done each one of us
Many favors in the past.   1270

Faust.   To confront this beast,
I'll need the fourfold spell:

Salamander shall glow,
Undine wind and flow,
Sylph fade away,   1275
Goblin toil all day.

Whoever's not cognizant
Of the four elements,
Of their capacities,
And of their properties,   1280
Can never be master
Over the spirits.

Fade into flames,
Salamander!
Merge your murmuring streams,   1285
Undine!
Shine with meteoric beauty,
Sylph!
Bring help to the house,
Incubus, Incubus!   1290
Come out and put an end to this!

None of the four
Can reside in the beast.
It's lying quite still and grinning at me;
I haven't hurt it yet.   1295
Well, you shall hear me
Cast a stronger spell.

Fellow, can you be
Some escapee from hell?

Observe this mark,[10]   1300
At which the dark
Infernal hordes must bow!

Now it's beginning to swell with bristling hairs.

Reprobate being!
Can you read the sign?   1305
Of One never generated,
Never articulated,
Diffused through the heavens,
Pierced by a spear irreverently?[11]

Banned behind the stove by my spells,   1310
Like an elephant it swells;
It's filling the whole room now
And seems to be dissolving into fog.
Don't rise to the ceiling!
Lie down here at your master's feet!   1315
You see that I'm not making empty threats.
I'm scorching you with sacred heat!
Do not await
The thrice-glowing light!
Do not await   1320
My most potent arts!

Mephistopheles (dressed as a wandering scholar and stepping out from
        behind the stove as the fog dissipates).
        What's all this noise? How can I be of service?

Faust. This, then, was the poodle's core?
        A wandering scholar? How amusing!

Mephistopheles. Let me salute a learned master!   1325
        You really had me sweating there.

10. The sign of the cross.
11. Cf. John 19:34.

Faust.   What do you call yourself?

Mephistopheles.   The question seems banal
            For one who so disdains the word;
            Who, far removed from all mere semblance,
            Trawls only in essential depths.   1330

Faust.   Among your sort it's easy to deduce
            The essence from the name;
            Your nature's all too evident
            When you're called God of Flies, Destroyer, Liar.
            Come now, who are you then?

Mephistopheles.   Part of the power   1335
            That constantly wants evil and constantly does good.

Faust.   And what's that riddle supposed to mean?

Mephistopheles. I am the spirit that continually negates!
            And rightly so, for all that comes to be
            Deserves to be annihilated;   1340
            It would be better, then, if nothing came to be.
            Thus everything that you call sin,
            Destruction, and in short, all you call evil,
            Is my native element.

Faust.   You call yourself a part and stand before me whole?   1345

Mephistopheles. I'm telling you the humble truth.
            Though humans, little worlds of folly,
            Are used to thinking they are wholes—
            I'm part of the part that once was all,
            Part of the dark that once gave birth to light,   1350
            That pompous light that now denies old mother night
            Her former rank, her realms of space,
            But can't prevail, because, no matter how it strives,
            Light's bound and glued to bodies.

It streams from bodies, makes them beautiful;   1355
A body will impede its passage,
And so, I hope, it won't be long,
Before both light and bodies are undone.

Faust.   I understand your noble duties!
You can't effect large-scale destruction,   1360
And so you start with something small.

Mephistopheles. I must admit I can't do much.
This clumsy world, this something,
That pits itself against my nothing—
In spite of all I've undertaken,   1365
I don't quite know how to get at it;
Through waves and storms, through quakes and fires—
In the end both sea and land remain at rest!
And that damn stuff, that brood of man and beast,
I can't affect them in the least: 1370
How many have I buried now!
New blood is always circulating,
And so it goes; it drives me quite insane!
A thousand seeds unfold,
From air and water, as well as from the soil,   1375
In dry and wet, in hot and cold!
And had I not laid claim to fire,
I would have nothing I could call my own.

Faust.   And so, against that ever stirring,
Creative, salutary might,   1380
You raise a cold and devilish fist,
Deviously clenched, but to no use!
Try something else,
Strange son of chaos!

Mephistopheles. We'll really have to think about it—   1385
But more of that in future visits!
May I take my leave for now?

Faust.   I don't see why you ask.
          Now that we are acquainted,
          Visit whenever you want.   1390
          Here is the window, there's the door,
          The chimney's also at your service.

Mephistopheles. I must confess a minor obstacle
          Stands in the way of my departure:
          The charm against witches on your doorsill—   1395

Faust.   That pentagram is troubling you?
          Come, tell me, son of hell,
          If that sign bans you, how did you get in?
          How was a spirit such as you deceived?

Mephistopheles. Look carefully! It's not well drawn;   1400
          One angle on the outside
          Is slightly open, as you see.

Faust.   A happy accident!
          And so you are my prisoner?
          That was sheer luck!   1405

Mephistopheles. The poodle didn't notice it when he jumped in,
          But now things look a little different:
          The devil can't get out of here.

Faust.   Why don't you just go through the window?

Mephistopheles. It is a law of devils and of ghosts: 1410
          Where they slip in, there too, they must go out.
          We're free to choose our entrances, but not our exits.

Faust.   Does hell itself have its laws too?
          I like that! I suppose, then, gentlemen,
          That one could make a pact, a binding one, with you?   1415

Mephistopheles. Whatever we promise, you'll get in full measure;
    You certainly won't be shortchanged.
    It's hard to settle such things quickly,
    And we'll discuss these matters soon;
    But now I really do entreat you,   1420
    To let me take my leave.

Faust.   But stay a moment longer,
    Give me the latest news before you go.

Mephistopheles. Let me leave! I'll come back soon,
    Then you can ask me anything you like.   1425

Faust.   I did not lure you in here;
    You stepped into the net yourself.
    Let him who holds the devil hold him tight!
    He won't catch him so easily a second time.

Mephistopheles. If that's your pleasure, I'm prepared   1430
    To stay and keep you company;
    But one condition: let me use my arts
    To help you pass the time in a worthy fashion.

Faust.   Feel free to choose; I'm happy to watch,
    As long as it is entertaining!   1435

Mephistopheles. Good friend, your senses will derive
    More profit from this hour,
    Than from a year's monotony.
    What these gentle spirits sing you,
    The lovely pictures that they bring you,   1440
    Are no empty magic show.
    With fragrant odors they'll delight you,
    And your tongue will taste sweet flavors;
    Touch will feel enchanted too.
    But no prelude is required,   1445
    We are assembled, let's begin!

Spirits.   Fade away, dark
         Vaults up above!
         Yield to the charming
         Blue ether's   1450
         Fond gaze!
         Let the dark clouds
         Dissipate quickly!
         Little stars twinkle,
         Milder suns   1455
         Shine on us now.
         Heavenly children's
         Numinous beauty
         Fluctuates, bows down,
         Floats gently by.   1460
         Inclination and longing
         Follow their flight;
         Fluttering ribbons
         Stream from their garments,
         Blanket the meadows,   1465
         Blanket the arbors,
         Where lost in their dreams,
         Lovers surrender,
         Vowing to love each other forever.
         Arbor on arbor!   1470
         Burgeoning tendrils!
         Grapes hanging heavy
         Plunge into baskets
         Of presses that crush them;
         Foaming new wines   1475
         Plummet in streams,
         Trickle through pure
         Gemstones and crystals,
         Leave the high slopes
         Lying behind them,   1480
         Spread out in lakes
         Around the delightful,
         Lush, greening hills.
         And all the birds
         Drink up this rapture,   1485
         Fly toward the sun,

Fly toward the shining,
Luminous islands
Rocking playfully
Over the waves;   1490
There we hear choirs
Singing exultantly,
There we see dancers
Whirling elatedly;
Out in the open   1495
All now disperse:
Some of them clambering
Over the heights,
Some of them swimming
Across the wide lakes,   1500
Some floating high in the air up above—
All toward life,
All toward the distance
Of loving stars,
Of gracious bliss.   1505

Mephistopheles. He's asleep! Well done, my delicate, airy boys!
        Loyally you sang your lullaby!
        I am indebted to you for this concert.
        You're not the man to hold the devil captive!
        Let sweet dream forms flutter around him;   1510
        Immerse him in an ocean of illusion—
        But to undo this doorway's spell,
        A rat's sharp tooth is what I need.
        This does not call for lengthy incantations;
        I hear one scampering there, and it will do my bidding. 1515

        The Lord of flies, of rats, and mice,
        The Lord of frogs, bedbugs, and lice
        Commands you to come boldly here
        And gnaw at the threshold of this door,
        Meanwhile he'll dab some oil on it—   1520
        Why there you come, scurrying out!
        Get straight to work! The point that banned me,
        Is at the front there, on the edge.

Just one more bite and you'll be done—
Now, Faust, dream on, until we meet again.   1525

Faust (waking up). Can I have been deceived again?
    The thronging spirits have all vanished.
    Was I just dreaming, then, about the devil,
    And that a poodle had escaped me?

Study

        (*Faust and Mephistopheles.*)

Faust.   Did someone knock? Come in! Who's here to plague
                me now?   1530

Mephistopheles. It's me.

Faust.   Come in!

Mephistopheles.   You have to say it three times.

Faust.   Come in then!

Mephistopheles.   That's what I like.
    I hope we'll get on well together!
    To chase away your dismal notions,
    I've come dressed as a noble cavalier: 1535
    My outfit's scarlet, trimmed in gold;
    I wear a cape of silk brocade,
    A cock's red feather in my hat,
    A long, sharp sword here at my side—
    And I advise you now, in short,   1540
    To don the same attire;
    Then, uninhibited and free, you'll soon
    Experience what life can be.

Faust.   In every outfit I am sure to feel
        The anguish of this narrow earthly life.   1545
        I am too old to play at games,
        Too young to have no wishes.
        What has the world to offer me?
        Thou shalt renounce! Renounce thou shalt!
        Yes, that commandment clangs   1550
        Incessantly in every ear;
        Our whole life long, each hour
        Repeats it hoarsely to us.
        In horror I awake each morning
        And would weep bitter tears   1555
        To see the day that in its course
        Will not fulfill *one* wish for me, not *one*,
        That will spoil any sense of pleasure
        With insistent little worries,
        Obstruct the lively breast's creations   1560
        With a thousand mundane trifles.
        And when night comes, then too,
        I'm never granted any rest;
        I lie down full of apprehensions;
        Wild dreams are sure to terrify me.   1565
        The god who dwells within my breast
        Can waken what lies deep inside me,
        But though he reigns over all my powers,
        He cannot move a thing outside me,
        And so existence is a burden;   1570
        I long for death; abhor this life.

Mephistopheles. Yet death is never an entirely welcome guest.

Faust.   Happy the victor of a glorious battle
        Whose brow death wreathes with bloody laurels!
        Happy the man death finds in a girl's warm arms,   1575
        After a fast and frantic dance!
        Had I only succumbed, enchanted and unsouled,
        To the power of that exalted spirit!

Mephistopheles. Yet someone did not finish drinking
      A brown potion that night.   1580

Faust. I see that you delight in espionage.

Mephistopheles. I'm not omniscient, but I know a lot.

Faust. If from that dreadful turmoil
      A sweet familiar sound recalled me,
      Beguiled vestigial childhood feelings,   1585
      By echoing that happy time,
      So now I curse all that ensnares the soul
      With alluring, playful gestures
      And holds it captive in this cave of sorrows
      With blinding powers of flattery!   1590
      Cursed first of all be high opinion,
      With which the mind entraps itself!
      Cursed be appearances that blind us,
      Thronging, pressing on our senses!
      Cursed be what whispers in our dreams,   1595
      Delusions of fame and a lasting name!
      Cursed be what flatters us as property,
      As wife and child, as plow and peasant!
      Cursed be Mammon, when with treasures
      He rouses us to do bold deeds,   1600
      And when he plumps soft pillows round us
      For indolent amusements.
      A curse upon the grape's sweet balm!
      A curse upon love's highest favors!
      A curse on hope! A curse on faith,   1605
      And cursed above all else be patience!

Chorus of Spirits (invisible). Alas!
      You have destroyed
      The lovely world
      With your strong fist;   1610
      It falls and shatters!
      A demigod has smashed it!
      We carry

The fragments into the nothingness,
And lament   1615
The beauty that's lost.
Mighty among
The sons of earth,
Build it anew
More splendidly;   1620
Build it within you!
Venture on
New paths of life
With clarity of mind,
And then new songs   1625
Will sound!

Mephistopheles. These little ones
Are my own.
Hear how they urge you
Precociously to joy and action!   1630
They wish to lure you
Out into the world,
Away from this isolation,
Out of this dull stagnation.

Stop toying with the bitter grief   1635
That's feeding on you like a vulture;
Even the worst society will let you feel
That you're as human as the next man.
Not that I intend
To shove you in among the rabble.   1640
I'm not especially distinguished,
But if you'd like to cast your lot with mine
And make your way through life with me,
Then I will gladly
Be yours at once.   1645
I'll be your companion,
And if I suit you,
I'll be your servant—your vassal too!

Faust. And what must I do, in return, for you?

Mephistopheles. Don't worry about that now—there's plenty
        of time.   1650

Faust.   No, no! The devil is an egoist
        And does not simply benefit
        Another for the sake of God.
        State your conditions clearly then—
        Such servants are a danger to the house.   1655

Mephistopheles. I'll bind myself to serve you *here*;
        At your behest I'll neither rest nor pause,
        And *yonder*, when we meet again,
        Then you must do the same for me.

Faust.   Your "yonder" does not bother me;   1660
        When you have smashed this world to pieces,
        Then let the next world come to be!
        For all my joys spring from this earth;
        This sun shines down on all my sorrows;
        If I can bring myself to part with them,   1665
        I do not care what happens next.
        I have no interest, none at all, in hearing
        Whether we'll hate and love there too,
        And whether in those spheres as well,
        There's an above and a below.   1670

Mephistopheles. Then in that spirit, why not risk it?
        Come, bind yourself, and soon you'll see
        My arts—they're sure to please.
        I'll show you things no human's ever seen.

Faust.   Poor devil, why, what would you show me?   1675
        Has your sort ever grasped
        The exalted striving of the human spirit?
        It's true that you have food that never satiates,
        Red gold that slips incessantly,
        Quicksilver-like, right through one's fingers;   1680
        You have a game that no one ever wins,

A girl who, as she's lying on my breast,
Already eyes another man seductively,
And that celestial pleasure, noble honor,
That fades as quickly as a shooting star.   1685
Show me the fruit that rots before you pick it,
The trees that sprout new leaves each day!

Mephistopheles. Assignments of that kind don't frighten me;
I'm happy to supply such treasures.
And yet, good friend, the time does come,   1690
When we want to savor something good in peace and quiet.

Faust.   If ever I lie down at peace upon a bed of ease,
Then let that be the end of me!
If your flattering words beguile me
And make me feel self-satisfied,   1695
If your pleasures can deceive me,
Then let that be my final day!
That's my wager!

Mephistopheles.   I accept!

Faust.   My hand on it!
If ever I say to the moment:
Stay a while! You are so fair!   1700
Then you can throw your chains around me!
Then I shall be quite glad to perish!
Then let the death-bell toll for me;
Then you will be released from service;
The clock can stop; its hand can drop—   1705
Let time itself be past for me!

Mephistopheles. Do think it over; we will not forget.

Faust.   You've every right to remember;
This is no reckless gamble on my part.
If I stand still, I am a vassal,   1710
Yours or another's—what do I care?

Mephistopheles. This very day I'll do my duty;
       I'll be your servant at the doctoral banquet.
       One small thing though! I usually request
       A line or two—in case of accident.   1715

Faust.   You pedant, you insist on something written too?
       Does a man's word mean nothing, then, to you?
       Isn't it sufficient that my spoken word
       Direct my days to all eternity?
       The world streams by in frantic haste—   1720
       Can a promise really hold me?
       Yet this illusion's anchored deep inside us,
       And who is willing to forgo it?
       Happy the man whose heart is pure and loyal,
       He makes no compromises he'll regret!   1725
       But a piece of parchment, signed and sealed,
       Is a ghost men shy away from.
       A word is dead as soon as it is written,
       Such is the majesty of wax and leather.
       Evil spirit, what do you want from me?   1730
       Metal, marble, parchment, paper?
       Am I to write with chisel, style, or quill?
       I leave the choice entirely to you.

Mephistopheles. You're overdoing it, you know,
       With your heated rhetoric.   1735
       Any little scrap will do;
       Just sign it with a tiny drop of blood.

Faust.   If you will be content with this,
       I'll go ahead with the charade.

Mephistopheles. Blood is a very special fluid.   1740

Faust.   Don't worry that I'll break this pact!
       To strive with all my power—
       Why that's exactly what I promise.
       I had inflated notions of my status;
       My rank is really here with you.   1745

That mighty spirit spurned me;
Nature has locked me out.
The thread of thought is broken;
Knowledge has long disgusted me.
Let us then soothe our glowing passions   1750
In depths of sensuality!
Set your wonders out before me,
But hide them in impenetrable cloths of magic!
Let us plunge into time's on-rushing current,
Into the rolling stream of events.   1755
Then pain and pleasure,
Success and failure
May alternate, as they will;
Only restlessly can a man be active.

Mephistopheles. There is no measure or limit set you.   1760
If you would like to have a taste of everything,
Grabbing a bite as you race by—
May what delights you do you good.
Please just dig in, and don't be shy!

Faust. You heard me, there's no talk of joy here.   1765
I dedicate myself to dissipation,
To painful pleasure, hate that loves, vexation
That invigorates. Cured of its thirst for knowledge,
My breast will not shut out a single sorrow,
And deep within me I'll enjoy   1770
All that's allotted to mankind;
My spirit will embrace the heights and depths,
I'll heap all human good and ill upon my breast,
Expand myself into the self of all humankind,
And, like it too, I'll founder in the end.   1775

Mephistopheles. Believe me, since I've chewed on this hard fare
For several thousand years,
That from the cradle to the grave no human
Has yet digested that old leaven!
Take it from one of us: this whole   1780
Is made for a god alone!

For he dwells in eternal light;
Into the dark he cast us out,
And your domain is day and night.

Faust.　　But I insist!

Mephistopheles.　　Alright then!　　　　　　　　1785
　　　　Just *one* thing troubles me, however:
　　　　Time is short, and art is long.
　　　　So I suggest you take some lessons.
　　　　Associate with some great poet
　　　　Whose thoughts range far and wide,　　　1790
　　　　And let him heap all noble qualities
　　　　Upon your worthy head—
　　　　The courage of a lion,
　　　　The swiftness of a stag,
　　　　The fiery blood of an Italian,　　　　　　1795
　　　　The northerner's tenacity.
　　　　Let him divulge to you the secrets
　　　　Of blending magnanimity and malice,
　　　　Or falling, full of youth's warm drives,
　　　　In love according to a plot.　　　　　　　1800
　　　　I'd like to know a man like that myself;
　　　　I'd call him Master Microcosm.

Faust.　　What am I, then, if it's not possible
　　　　To gain humanity's high crown,
　　　　Toward which all my senses strain?　　　1805

Mephistopheles.　In the end you are—what you are.
　　　　Wear a wig with a million curls,
　　　　Wear the highest platform shoes,
　　　　You'll still remain just what you are.

Faust.　　I feel how futile it has been　　　　　1810
　　　　To seize the treasures of the human intellect,
　　　　And in the end, when I sit down,
　　　　No new strength wells within me;

I'm not one hair's breadth higher,
Not one bit nearer to the infinite. 1815

Mephistopheles. Good sir, you look at things
The way that people generally do;
We'll need to be far more perceptive,
So that life's joys do not escape us.
Hang it all! It's true that hands and feet 1820
And head and tail are yours;
But everything I make good use of,
Is it not mine as well?
If I can buy six stallions,
Are not their powers mine? 1825
I speed right up, I've got it made,
Running on twenty-four strong legs.
So quick! Forget your rumination,
And come into the world with me!
I'll tell you this: a man who speculates 1830
Is like a beast that stays on barren ground;
It's led in circles by an evil spirit,
While fresh green grass is growing all around.

Faust. But how shall we begin?

Mephistopheles. By getting out of here.
What sort of torture chamber is this? 1835
What kind of life is it
To bore yourself and young men stiff?
Leave that to your complacent colleagues!
Why plague yourself with threshing straw?
The best things that you know 1840
You cannot tell those dear boys anyway.
I hear one now, out in the corridor!

Faust. I cannot bring myself to see him.

Mephistopheles. The poor boy has been waiting quite a while,
He shouldn't go without some consolation. 1845

Why come, give me your cap and gown;
This costume ought to suit me perfectly.
   (*He changes his clothes.*)
And now, just trust my natural aptitude!
I need a little quarter-hour,
While you get ready for a lovely trip!   1850

   (*Exit Faust.*)

Mephistopheles (*in Faust's long gown*). Yes, do despise reason and
            learning,
      The highest human powers,
      And let the spirit of deception
      Confirm you in its dazzling tricks of conjury;
      Then you'll be absolutely mine—   1855
      Fate has given him a spirit
      That presses on without restraint,
      Whose overhasty striving
      Overleaps all earthly joys.
      I'll drag him through a riotous existence,   1860
      Through dull, flat insignificance,
      I'll make him wriggle, twitch, and stick,[12]
      And food and drink shall hover just beyond
      The greedy lips of his insatiability.
      In vain he'll beg refreshment—   1865
      And even if he had not given himself
      Over to the devil, he would have to perish!

   (*A Student enters.*)

Student. I've only recently arrived;
      I've come to pay you my respects
      And make the acquaintance of a man   1870
      Whose name all mention reverently.

Mephistopheles. Your manners are delightful!
      But as you see, I am a man like others.
      Have you inquired elsewhere?

---

12.   Perhaps an image of an insect getting caught in honey, or a bird in bird-lime.

Student. I beg you, take me on!   1875
    I'm young and full of spirit,
    Not short of money, healthy too;
    My mother wanted me to stay at home;
    I'd like to get a decent education.

Mephistopheles. Why then, this is the very place for you.   1880

Student. Honestly, I'd like to leave already:
    Within these walls, these hallways,
    I don't feel right at all.
    The space is so confined;
    There's nothing green in sight, no, not one tree,   1885
    And in the classrooms on those benches
    I lose my hearing, sight, and mind.

Mephistopheles. You will get used to it.
    So too, at first a child's reluctant
    To take its mother's breast,   1890
    But soon it nurses eagerly.
    So too, each day you'll grow more eager
    To drink from wisdom's breasts.

Student. I'll hang about her neck with joy,
    If you'll just tell me where to find her.   1895

Mephistopheles. Before you continue, please declare
    What faculty you've chosen.

Student. I want to become truly learned;
    I'd like to grasp all that's on earth
    And in the heavens too,   1900
    Human knowledge, yes, and nature.

Mephistopheles. You're certainly on the right track there;
    Just don't let anything distract you.

Student.   Oh I'm committed, soul and body;
           Although, you know, I would enjoy   1905
           A bit of freedom and some leisure
           On warm and sunny days in summer.

Mephistopheles.   Use your time well, it goes by quickly;
           Order and method are essential.
           Therefore, dear friend, I would advise you   1910
           To take a course in logic first.[13]
           For there your mind will be well trained
           And tightly strapped in Spanish boots,[14]
           So that in future it will creep
           More cautiously along the paths of thought,   1915
           No longer straying everywhere
           Like a will-o'-the-wisp, now here, now there.[15]
           They'll take some days to teach you
           That what you used to do in a single stroke,
           As easy as eating and drinking,   1920
           Takes several steps—one, two, and three!
           Indeed the factory of our thoughts
           Is like a master weaver's loom:
           One treadle shifts a thousand threads;
           The shuttles bolt, now back, now forth;   1925
           The threads flow imperceptibly;
           A single action joins a thousand strands;
           Here the philosopher steps in
           And demonstrates it must be so:
           The first is so, the second so,   1930
           Therefore the third and fourth are so,
           And if steps one and two aren't true,
           Then three and four no longer are.

13.   In his autobiography, *Poetry and Truth*, Goethe recalls his own time as a student in Leipzig: "As for the study of logic, it seemed very strange to me, that I was supposed to tear apart, separate, and as it were, destroy operations of the intellect I had performed with the greatest ease since childhood, in order to learn how to use them correctly." WA, part I, vol. 27, p. 53.

14.   An instrument of torture named for its use in the Spanish Inquisition.

15.   A will-o'-the-wisp or *ignis fatuus* is a mysterious light said to lead travelers off the path into marshy ground.

Students all over praise his conclusion;
Not one of them's become a weaver.   1935
Who would describe and know a living thing,
Tries first to drive its spirit out;
Then he has its parts in hand,
But lacks, alas, the vital bond.
Encheiresin naturae chemistry calls this;[16]   1940
It mocks itself and does not know it.

Student. I don't quite understand you.

Mephistopheles. You'll find it easier once you've learned
    To reduce all things to principles
    And classify them systematically.   1945

Student. All that just makes me feel so stupid,
    As if I had a mill-wheel turning in my head.

Mephistopheles. And after this, before all other subjects,
    You must apply yourself to metaphysics!
    Then see that with deep thoughts you grasp   1950
    What will not fit inside the human brain—
    For what goes in and for what doesn't,
    Some splendid word will be at your disposal.
    But most of all, the first semester,
    Make sure that you are organized.   1955
    You'll have five classes every day,
    See that you're present when the bell rings!
    Prepare for each class in advance;
    Study the appointed paragraphs,
    So that you'll see more clearly: 1960
    He only says what's right there in the book.
    Nevertheless, you must take notes as diligently,
    As if the Holy Spirit were dictating to you!

---

16.   Literally a "taking in hand" or "undertaking of nature." In a letter of January 21, 1832 to the chemist H. W. F. Wackenroder, Goethe speaks of nature's "secret *encheiresis*, by means of which she creates and promotes life" and which finally forces us to admit that there is something beyond our powers of investigation. WA, part IV, vol. 49, p. 210.

Student. You will not have to tell me that again!
        I see that what you say's extremely useful;   1965
        What's written down in black and white,
        You carry home, assured you've got it!

Mephistopheles. But come now, choose a faculty!

Student. I'd never get used to law.

Mephistopheles. That's something I can't hold against you;   1970
        I know exactly what that subject's like.
        Statutes and laws are handed down
        Eternally, like a contagion;
        They drag themselves from one generation to the next
        And shuffle along from place to place.   1975
        Reason becomes absurd, a kind deed harmful.
        Take pity on us heirs!
        As for that right that we are born with,
        Of that, alas, there's never any talk.

Student. My aversion grows with every word you say.   1980
        How fortunate your students are!
        Why now I'm almost leaning toward theology!

Mephistopheles. I wouldn't want to mislead you.
        It's hard for students of theology
        To avoid the paths of heresy: 1985
        This discipline contains a lot of hidden venom,
        Which one can easily mistake for medicine.
        Here too, you'd best attend *one* master's lectures,
        And swear by every word you hear him say.
        And in general—stick to words!   1990
        Then you'll pass safely through the gates that guard
        Certainty's inviolable temple.

Student. And yet a concept must accompany each word.

Mephistopheles. Yes, but do not agonize too much about it:
    Just where a concept may prove hard to find, 1995
    An opportune expression often comes to mind.
    With words you can debate exquisitely,
    With words you can set up a system,
    Words lend themselves to ready credence,
    And from a word you can't steal one iota. 2000

Student. Excuse me for detaining you with questions,
    But I must trouble you a little longer.
    Do you have any potent words to share
    Concerning medicine?
    Three years pass quickly, 2005
    And Lord! The field is far too wide.
    If someone points you in the right direction,
    You can begin to feel your way.

Mephistopheles (to himself). I'm getting tired of this dry tone
    And need to play the devil once again. 2010
    (Aloud.) The spirit of medicine's not hard to grasp;
    Examine the world, both great and small,
    From top to bottom,
    Then let it go just as God pleases.
    Extensive studies are a waste of time; 2015
    Each masters only what he can;
    But he who seizes the moment
    Has got it made!
    Then again, you're fairly good-looking—
    Bold enough too, it seems— 2020
    And if you simply trust your instincts,
    Other souls will trust you too.
    Above all learn to handle women;
    Their eternal aches and pains,
    Though thousandfold, 2025
    Can all be cured with *one* straightforward remedy;
    Treat them half-decently,
    And soon you'll have them under your thumb.
    A title first—to reassure her
    That your skills far surpass the skills of others, 2030

And then—to set her mind at ease—some gentle probing
For assets that would take another years to find;
Tenderly you feel her pulse,
And casting sly and fiery glances,
You freely grasp her slender waist   2035
To check how tightly she is laced.

Student. That sounds much better! Now I get it!

Mephistopheles. All theory, dear friend, is grey,
And green the golden tree of life.

Student. I swear, this seems to be a dream.   2040
May I impose on you some other time
And hear the rest of your great wisdom?

Mephistopheles. I'm always glad to be of service.

Student. It's quite impossible for me to leave
Before I've handed you my album.   2045
Do me a favor, please, and sign it!

Mephistopheles. Certainly. (*He writes and gives it back.*)

Student (reading). Eritis sicut Deus scientes bonum et malum.[17]
        (*He closes the album reverently and takes his leave.*)

Mephistopheles. Heed the old saying and my relative, the serpent—
Some day you're sure to shudder at your godlikeness!   2050

        (*Faust enters.*)

Faust. Where then shall we go now?

Mephistopheles.   Wherever you would like.
We'll see the small world first and then the great.

---

17. "You will be like God, knowing good and evil" (Genesis 3:5).

How you'll enjoy and profit from
This course—without paying any tuition!

Faust.   Yet with my professorial beard and all,   2055
The experiment is bound to fail;
I've never had your easy-going ways.
I never got on well with people.
I feel so small in front of others;
I'll always seem quite out of place.   2060

Mephistopheles.   Good friend, it will all work out;
Just trust your instincts, and you'll soon learn how to live.

Faust.   How will we get away from here?
Where are your horses, groom, and carriage?

Mephistopheles.   We'll just spread out my cloak like this;   2065
It will transport us through the air.
But bear in mind that it's a daring move—
Please do not pack too large a bag.
I will prepare some flammable air
To lift us off the ground in style.   2070
If we are light enough, we will rise quickly;
Congratulations on your new career!

Auerbach's Cellar in Leipzig

(A group of drinking companions.)

Frosch.   Will no one drink? Or joke, or laugh?
I'll teach you all to make long faces!
You're like a bundle of wet straw today,   2075
And generally you burn so brightly.

Brander.   Well that's your fault; you're not contributing
Your usual dumb jokes and dirty tricks.

Frosch (dumping a glass of wine on Brander's head).
    Well then I'll give you both at once!

Brander.   You double ass!

Frosch. You asked for it; you told me to!   2080

Siebel. Get lost, if you are going to quarrel!
    Open your throats and sing—or drink—a round!
    Shout it out! Hey there! Hallo!

Altmayer. Oh help, he's killing me!
    Some cotton quick! He'll burst my eardrums.

Siebel. It's only when the vault reverberates,   2085
    That you can feel the full force of a bass.

Frosch. That's right, and out the door with anyone
    Who takes offense! La, trala lala la!

Altmayer. La, trala lala la!

Frosch.   Our voices are in tune.
    (Sings.) The dear old Holy Roman Empire,   2090
    How do its limbs still hang together?

Brander. A rotten song! A dissolute, political,
    And feeble song! Give thanks to God each morning
    That you don't have to rule the Empire!
    I at least am highly grateful   2095
    That I'm not Emperor or Chancellor.
    But we should have a ruler too—
    Let us elect a pope.
    You know what sort of qualities
    Tip the balance and advance a man's career.   2100

Frosch (singing). Sweet nightingale arise and take
   Ten thousand greetings to my love.

Siebel. No greetings to your love! I cannot stand that stuff!

Frosch. Greetings and kisses to my love! You cannot stop me!
   (Sings.) Open the latch! The night is still.   2105
   Open the latch! Your lover's waiting.
   Shut the latch! For morning's breaking.

Siebel. Yes sing, oh sing, extol and praise her!
   When it's my turn to laugh I'll do so.
   She led me along; she'll do the same to you. 2110
   Let some lusty goblin be her lover,
   Who'll fool around with her at the crossroads;
   Let some old buck, returning from the Blocksberg,[18]
   Bleat her good-night, as he goes galloping by.
   A decent fellow made of flesh and blood   2115
   Is far too good for a minx like that.
   If I ever hear you sing of greetings again,
   I'll send some smashing through her window-pane!

Brander (banging on the table).
   Attention everyone! Attention! Listen,
   You must admit that I know how to live;   2120
   There are some lovers here among us,
   And people of such noble status
   Deserve a song befitting their position.
   Listen closely! This one's the latest fashion!
   Join in the chorus; sing out lustily!   2125

   (Sings.) There lived a rat down in the cellar,
   Could only stomach fat and butter,
   Soon she'd acquired a little tummy

---

18. The Blocksberg or Brocken is the highest mountain in the Harz mountain range. According to legend, it is the site of the witches' sabbath on Walpurgis Night. (See the note to line 2590.)

Just like dear Doctor Luther.
The cook put out some poison for her,   2130
And soon the rat felt so confined,
As if she'd got love in her belly.

Chorus (jubilantly). As if she'd got love in her belly!

Brander. She raced around; she raced outside;
She drank from every puddle;   2135
She gnawed, she chewed the house to bits—
Nothing could stop her frantic fits;
But soon enough the poor beast was through,
Performed a *salto mortale* or two,
As if she'd got love in her belly.   2140

Chorus. As if she'd got love in her belly!

Brander. And in her fright she ran inside,
Into the kitchen, in broad daylight.
Fell at the stove and twitched and lay,
And gasped for air most piteously.   2145
Her killer only laughed out loud:
"She's whistling one last tune, you know,
As if she'd got love in her belly."

Chorus. As if she'd got love in her belly!

Siebel. How these stupid fellows enjoy it!   2150
You'd think it was an art
To scatter poison for a rat!

Brander. I suppose that rats find favor with you?

Altmayer. That pot-belly with his bald pate!
Misfortune's made him tame and meek,   2155
And in that swollen rat he sees
The natural image of himself.

(Faust and Mephistopheles enter.)

Mephistopheles. The main thing is to get you out
   Into some lively company,
   So you'll see how to take life easy.   2160
   For these good folks each day's a holiday.
   With little sense and great enjoyment,
   Each dances in a narrow circle,
   The way a kitten chases its own tail.
   As long as their heads are not aching,   2165
   As long as landlords extend them credit,
   They are content and have no cares.

Brander. Why, look at them, they're travelers,
   You can tell by their foreign ways;
   Those two have not been here one hour.   2170

Frosch. How right you are! I'll sing the praises of my Leipzig!
   It is a little Paris and cultivates its people.

Siebel. What sort of men do you think these strangers are?

Frosch. Leave it to me! Once they have had a glass,
   I'll worm their secrets gently out of them,   2175
   Extract them just like baby teeth.
   I'd guess they're of a noble house:
   They look dissatisfied and proud.

Brander. Con artists of some sort, I'll wager!

Altmayer. Perhaps.

Frosch.   Watch me, I'll squeeze it out of them! 2180

Mephistopheles (to Faust). Such common folk can't sense the devil—
   Not even if he has them by the collar.

Faust. Greetings, gentlemen!

Siebel.   Our thanks, and greetings in return.
    (Softly, looking at Mephistopheles from the side.)
    Why is he limping on one foot?

Mephistopheles. May we join you? In lieu of a good drink—   2185
    For it's impossible to get one here—
    Your company will soon refresh us.

Altmayer. You seem somewhat fastidious, sir.

Frosch. I guess you were late leaving Rippach?
    Did you stay and dine with Master Jackass?   2190

Mephistopheles. We went right by his place today!
    Last time we stopped and talked to him.
    He told us all about his cousins,
    Sends his regards to each of you.
    (He bows to Frosch.)

Altmayer (softly). You see? He gets the joke!

Siebel.   A clever customer!   2195

Frosch. Just wait, I'll pay him back!

Mephistopheles. We heard, if I am not mistaken,
    A most accomplished choir of voices singing?
    Indeed, a song would surely resonate
    Exquisitely from such a vaulted ceiling.   2200

Frosch. Are you a virtuoso then?

Mephistopheles. Oh no! My voice is weak, although I love to sing.

Altmayer. Give us a song!

Mephistopheles.   As many as you want.

Siebel. As long as it's a brand-new piece!

Mephistopheles. We've just come back from Spain,   2205
    The lovely land of wine and song.
    (*Sings.*) Long ago there lived a king,
    Who had a giant flea—

Frosch. Listen to him! A flea! Did you get that?
    A flea's a tidy sort of guest.   2210

Mephistopheles (singing). Long ago there lived a king,
    Who had a giant flea;
    He loved it very dearly,
    As dearly as a son.
    And so he called his tailor,   2215
    And when the tailor came,
    He bade him cut a jacket
    And breeches for the squire!

Brander. Just don't forget to tell the tailor
    To measure the flea precisely,   2220
    And, if he values his life at all,
    To see the breeches hang correctly!

Mephistopheles. In velvet then and satin,
    The flea was soon arrayed,
    With medals on his jacket,   2225
    And a distinguished cross.
    Then he became a minister,
    And got a great big star,
    And all his little brothers
    Became great men at court.   2230

    At court the lords and ladies
    All suffered agonies;
    The queen and lady-in-waiting
    Were bitten by those fleas;
    They weren't allowed to squash them,   2235

They weren't allowed to scratch.
But hey! We catch and crush them,
Whenever they bite us.

Chorus (jubilantly). But hey! We catch and crush them,
          Whenever they bite us.   2240

Frosch.   Bravo! Bravo! That was beautiful!

Siebel.   And may that be the fate of every flea!

Brander. Pinch your fingers and squeeze them tight!

Altmayer. Long live freedom! Long live wine!

Mephistopheles. I'd like to raise my glass and drink a toast
                    to freedom,   2245
          If only you had wines of better quality.

Siebel.   Oh please, let's not hear that again!

Mephistopheles. I'm just afraid the landlord might complain,
          Or I would serve these valued guests
          Some of the best my cellar has to offer.   2250

Siebel.   Just bring it here! I'll take the blame.

Frosch.   If you produce good wine, we'll sing your praises.
          But please, make sure your samples aren't too small.
          I cannot taste them properly,
          Unless I have my mouth quite full.   2255

Altmayer (softly). They're from the Rhineland, I can tell.

Mephistopheles. Bring me a drill!

Brander.   Whatever for?
      Surely you don't have casks outside the door?

Altmayer. The landlord keeps a box of tools back there.

Mephistopheles (taking the drill and addressing Frosch).
      So tell me now, what would you like to try?   2260

Frosch. What do you mean? Do you have a selection?

Mephistopheles. You're free to choose what kind you like.

Altmayer (to Frosch). Licking your lips already, are you?

Frosch. Well then! If I'm to choose, something from the Rhine.
      One's native land affords the choicest gifts.   2265

*Mephistopheles (drilling a hole in the edge of the table where Frosch is
      sitting).*
      Bring me some wax, we'll need some stoppers in a minute!

Altmayer. That's one of those old conjuror's tricks.

Mephistopheles (to Brander). And you?

Brander.   I'd like champagne;
      Make sure it's good and bubbly too!

      *(Mephistopheles drills. In the meantime someone
      has made wax stoppers and plugs the holes.)*

Brander. Sometimes one can't steer clear of foreign products;   2270
      What's good is often far from us.
      True Germans cannot stand the French,
      But drink their wines quite happily.

Siebel (*as Mephistopheles comes over to his place at the table*).
  I must admit, dry wine does not appeal to me—
  Give me a glass of something really sweet!   2275

Mephistopheles (*drilling*). In an instant Tokay shall flow for you.

Altmayer. Come, gentlemen, and look me in the face!
  It's obvious you're playing tricks on us.

Mephistopheles. No, not at all! With such distinguished guests
  That would be taking quite a risk.   2280
  Quick! Come now, let me know!
  What wine may I serve you?

Altmayer. Any one at all! Don't waste time asking.

Mephistopheles (*with strange gestures, after all the holes have been
    drilled and plugged*).
  Vines bear grapes,
  And goats wear horns;   2285
  Wine is fluid, vines are wood,
  A wooden table yields wine too.
  A deep glimpse into nature's kingdom!
  A miracle, if you have faith!

  Now pull the stoppers out and drink!   2290

All (*as they remove the stoppers and the wine each requested flows
    into his glass*).
  What a beautiful fountain flows for us!

Mephistopheles. Be careful, don't let any spill!

  (*They drink repeatedly.*)

All (*singing*). We're happy little cannibals,
  As happy as five hundred pigs!

Mephistopheles. The people are free, and see how happy they are!   2295

Faust.   I'd like to leave now.

Mephistopheles. But watch this first, for bestiality
     Will soon reveal itself in all its glory.

Siebel (drinks carelessly; the wine spills on the ground and becomes a flame).
     Help! Fire! Help! All hell is burning!

Mephistopheles (addressing the flame). Lie still, congenial element!   2300
     (*To the company.*) This was just a drop of purgatorial fire.

Siebel.   What's that supposed to mean? You'll pay for this!
     I guess you don't know who we are.

Frosch.   You'd better not try that again!

Altmayer. We'd best discreetly tell him to get out of here.   2305

Siebel.   What, sir? Do you really dare
     To try that hocus-pocus here?

Mephistopheles. Quiet, you old wine-jug!

Siebel.   Broomstick!
     Do you think you can insult us too?

Brander. You'll soon feel blows come raining down on you!   2310

Altmayer (pulls a stopper out of the table and flames leap out at him).
     I'm burning! I'm burning!

Siebel.   It's sorcery! And sorcerers are
     Outside the law! So beat them with impunity!

(They draw their knives and go after Mephistopheles.)

Mephistopheles *(with solemn gestures).* Misleading words, deceptive
      shapes,
    Distract the mind, transform the place!
    Let them be here and there at once!   2315

(They stand in astonishment and stare at one another.)

Altmayer. Where am I? What a lovely country!

Frosch. Vineyards! I can't believe my eyes!

Siebel.   And grapes too, right at hand!

Brander. Here under these green branches,
    Look at this vine! Look at this grape!

    *(He grabs Siebel by the nose. The rest grab each
    other by the nose and raise their knives.)*

Mephistopheles *(with similar gestures).* Error, take your blindfold
      from their eyes!   2320
    And you, mark well what jokes the devil plays.

    *(He disappears with Faust; the companions
    draw back from each other.)*

Siebel. What's going on?

Altmayer.   How's this?

Frosch.   Was that your nose?

Brander *(to Siebel).* And I'm holding yours in my hand!

Altmayer. That was a shock that went right through me!
    Get me a chair, I'm going to faint!   2325

Frosch. Incredible! Tell me, what happened?

Siebel.   Where is that fellow? If I get wind of him,
       He will not get away from here alive!

Altmayer. Going out the cellar door—
       I saw him—riding on an empty cask—   2330
       My feet feel heavy as lead.
          (*Turning toward the table.*)
       Oh my! Do you suppose the wine's still flowing?

Siebel.   It was all false—a lie, mere semblance.

Frosch.   And yet it seemed to me that I was drinking wine.

Brander. And what about those grapes?   2335

Altmayer. Who says you can't believe in miracles!

Witch's Kitchen

       (*A large cauldron hangs over the fire on a low hearth.
       Various shapes appear in the steam rising from the
       cauldron. A female meerkat is sitting by the cauldron,
       skimming off the foam and making sure the cauldron
       doesn't boil over. The male sits nearby with their
       offspring and warms himself. The walls and ceiling are
       decorated with strange witch's utensils.*)

       (*Faust and Mephistopheles.*)

Faust.   This crazy sorcery's repulsive!
       How can you promise I'll recover
       In this ridiculous chaos?
       Did I ask for advice from some old hag?   2340
       And will this foul concoction
       Take thirty years off from my body?
       Is this the best that you can do?
       My hopes have all evaporated.
       Has nature or a noble mind   2345
       Not found a better medicine than this?

Mephistopheles. Well, now you're talking sense again, my friend!
    Natural methods of rejuvenation do exist,
    But they are written in a different book
    And constitute a most peculiar chapter.   2350

Faust. I want to know them.

Mephistopheles.   Fine! There's a method that's free;
    It doesn't require doctors or magic:
    Go straight out into the fields,
    Begin to hoe the ground and dig,
    Confine yourself and all your thoughts   2355
    To that restricted sphere,
    Sustain yourself with simple foods,
    Live as a beast with beasts, and don't think it beneath you
    To spread your dung on fields that you will harvest;
    That's the best way, believe me,   2360
    To stay young eighty years or more!

Faust. I am not used to that, could never bring myself
    To take a shovel in my hands.
    That narrow life would never suit me.

Mephistopheles. But then the witch must do the job.   2365

Faust. Why does it have to be that hag?
    Why can't you brew the drink yourself?

Mephistopheles. A nice way that would be to spend my time!
    When I could be off building devil's bridges![19]
    Science and art are not sufficient;   2370
    Such work demands tremendous patience.
    A quiet spirit toils industriously for years;
    It's time alone that makes this liquor potent.

19. These are medieval bridges that according to legend—usually because they exhibit remarkable feats of engineering—were the outcome of some kind of pact between the master-builder and the devil. One of the most famous is the bridge at the St. Gotthard Pass in Switzerland, which Goethe visited in 1779.

And all that goes into the process
Is strange and wonderful as well!   2375
Although the devil taught her how,
The devil cannot make it now.
    (*He sees the animals.*)
What delicate breed is this?
Look, she's the maid and he's the servant!
(*To the animals.*) It seems your mistress isn't home?   2380

The Animals. At a party,
        Out of the house,
        Out the chimney!

Mephistopheles. And how long does she roam on such occasions?

Animals. As long as it takes us to warm our paws.   2385

Mephistopheles (*to Faust*). How do you like these dainty creatures?

Faust.   Disgusting little things.

Mephistopheles. Not at all. This is the very kind
        Of conversation I like most.
        (*To the animals.*) But tell me, you damned puppets,   2390
        What is that brew you're stirring there?

The Animals. Thin soup for beggars.

Mephistopheles. You won't be short of clientele.

The Male Meerkat (*coming over and fawning on Mephistopheles*).
        Oh throw the dice
        And make me rich,   2395
        And let me win!
        It's all poorly arranged,
        But if I had money,
        They'd say I was sane.

Mephistopheles. How fortunate this ape would think himself,   2400
    If he could play the lottery!

       (In the meantime the young meerkats have been playing
       with a large globe, which they now roll forward.)

The Male Meerkat. This is the world;
    It rises and falls
    And rolls on and on;
    It sounds like glass—   2405
    How fast that shatters!
    It's hollow inside.
    But here it glistens
    And seems to promise:
    I'm full of life!   2410
    My beloved son,
    Keep away from it!
    You shall surely die!
    What's made of clay
    Will break in pieces.   2415

Mephistopheles. What's that sieve for?

The Male Meerkat (taking it down).
    If you were a thief,
    I'd know right away.
      (He runs to the female meerkat and
      lets her look through it.)
    Look through the sieve!
    Do you recognize the thief,   2420
    Although you dare not name him?

Mephistopheles (approaching the fire). And this pot?

Both Meerkats. Silly idiot!
    Doesn't know what a pot
    Or a cauldron is!   2425

Mephistopheles. Uncivil beast!

Male Meerkat. Here, take this whisk[20]
        And sit in that chair!

    (He makes Mephistopheles sit down.)

Faust (who has been standing in front of a mirror the entire time,
            alternately moving toward it and away from it).
        What heavenly image do I see
        Appearing in this magic mirror!   2430
        O love, lend me the swiftest of your wings,
        And lead me to the regions she inhabits!
        Alas, as soon as I move from this spot,
        Or if I venture one bit closer,
        She fades into obscurity!   2435
        How beautiful this woman's image is!
        Can woman be so beautiful?
        And must I see in this reclining body
        The epitome of all the heavens?
        Can such a being dwell on earth?   2440

Mephistopheles. Well, if a god spends six days hard at work
        And then congratulates himself on his performance,
        Something intelligent should come of it!
        Feel free to feast your eyes on her,
        For I can ferret out such treasures—   2445
        Happy is he who's destined
        To lead her home as his bride!
          (Faust keeps on looking in the mirror.
          Mephistopheles, stretching out in the chair and
          playing with the whisk, continues speaking.)
        Here, like a king upon his throne, I sit
        And hold my scepter; all that's missing is a crown.

The Animals (who have been making all sorts of peculiar movements,
            with a great cry, bring Mephistopheles a crown.)
        The crown has a crack—   2450
        Be good enough please
        To plaster it with sweat and blood!

---

20. Alternately, "feather duster" or "fly swatter."

(They handle the crown awkwardly and break it in
two. They prance around with the two pieces.)
Now it is broken!
We talk and we look,
We hear and we rhyme—   2455

Faust *(still facing the mirror).* I'm losing my mind.

Mephistopheles *(pointing to the animals).* My head's beginning to
         spin a little too.

The Animals. And when by some chance,
         The words happen to suit,
         We call it a thought!   2460

Faust *(as above).* A fire's beginning to burn inside me!
         Let's leave at once!

Mephistopheles *(in the same posture).* Oh well, you must at least admit,
         That they are pretty honest poets.

         (The cauldron, which the female meerkat has ignored,
         begins to boil over; a great flame bursts forth and
         shoots out the chimney. The Witch comes flying
         down through the flame with a terrible cry.)

The Witch. Ow! Ow! Ow! Ow!   2465
         Damned beast! Cursed brute!
         To abandon your cauldron and scald your mistress!
         Cursed beast!
         (Catching sight of Faust and Mephistopheles.)
         What have we here?
         Who are you there?   2470
         What do you want?
         Who crept in here?
         May fires of hell
         Afflict your bones!

(Plunging the skimming-ladle into the cauldron, she
sprays flames in the direction of Faust, Mephistopheles,
and the animals. The animals whimper.)

Mephistopheles *(reversing the whisk he's holding and smashing jars*
                and pots).
        In two! In two!   2475
        There lies your brew!
        There lies your glass!
        It's just a joke,
        The beat, you ass,
        To your pathetic tune.   2480
          (As the witch steps back full of fury and horror.)
        Do you recognize me now? You bag of bones!
        Do you recognize your lord and master?
        What's to stop me now from thrashing you,
        From smashing you and your meowing spirits!
        Have you lost all respect for this red doublet?   2485
        Can't you recognize the bright cock's feather?
        Have I by any chance come in disguise?
        Am I supposed to announce myself?

The Witch. Please, sir, excuse the rude reception!
        But I don't see a cloven hoof.   2490
        And where, pray tell, are your two ravens?

Mephistopheles. I'll let it go this time;
        It's been a while, that's true,
        Since we last saw each other.
        Culture, which licks all corners of the world,   2495
        Has stretched its tongue and touched the devil too;
        The phantom of the north is seen no more.
        Where can one find horns now, or tail and claws?
        As for the hoof, though I can't do without it,
        Nowadays people find it offensive;   2500
        So for some years I have been using
        Padded stockings, as other young men do.

The Witch *(dancing).* I'm going out of my mind with glee—
        Can it really be Squire Satan that I see?

Mephistopheles. Woman, that name is now forbidden! 2505

The Witch. But why? What harm has it done you?

Mephistopheles. Oh, it's been relegated to the realm of fables,
    Though people are no better off without it;
    The Evil One is gone, but evil ones remain.
    Just call me "Baron," that will do; 2510
    I am a nobleman, like other noblemen.
    But if you've any doubts about my lineage,
    Here's my hereditary coat of arms!
      (He makes an obscene gesture.)

The Witch (laughing immoderately). Ha! Ha! That's just your style!
    You always were a dirty rascal! 2515

Mephistopheles (to Faust). Learn a few tricks from me, my friend!
    This is the way to handle witches.

The Witch. Now tell me, gentlemen, what's your command?

Mephistopheles. A tumbler of your famous juice!
    And I will need the oldest vintage; 2520
    Its age will make it doubly potent.

The Witch. Glad to oblige! I've got a bottle here,
    So old it's lost its stench completely;
    I sometimes take a nip from it myself
    And would be glad to give you some. 2525
      (Softly.)
    But if this man does not prepare himself
    Before he drinks, he'll die within the hour, you know.

Mephistopheles. He's a good friend, and it will do him good;
    I'd like him to have the best you've got.
    Now draw your circle, recite your spells, 2530
    Give him a tumbler full of it!

*(The Witch, making peculiar gestures, draws a
circle and puts strange things in it; in the meantime
the glasses begin to ring, and the cauldrons to
sound and make music. Finally she brings out a
large book and sets the meerkats in the circle. They
have to serve as her lectern and hold torches for
her. She beckons Faust to come over to her.)*

Faust. Tell me, what is the point of this?
These crazy antics, these demented gestures,
The whole disgusting masquerade—
I know them well and I detest them.   2535

Mephistopheles. Yes, it's a farce and utterly absurd!
Why must you always be so serious?
The doctor has to do a little hocus-pocus,
Before the juice can do you good.

(He makes Faust step into the circle.)

The Witch *(beginning to declaim emphatically from her book).*
Just listen then!   2540
From one make ten,
Get rid of two,
Now make three even,
You'll be rich soon.
Let four be gone!   2545
From five and six,
So says the witch,
Make seven and eight,
Then you are done:
And nine is one,   2550
And ten is none.
That is the way we witches reckon.

Faust. I think the poor old thing's delirious.

Mephistopheles. She's nowhere near the end of it,
The whole book sounds like that, I know it well;   2555
I've wasted quite a bit of time with it,

For total contradiction mystifies
Wise men and fools in equal measure.
This art is old and new, my friend,
For there's a long tradition   2560
Of using three and one, and one and three,
To multiply not truth, but heresy.
They prate and preach incessantly;
Why get involved in foolish disputations?
It's just man's custom to assume the words he hears   2565
Must yield to some interpretation.

The Witch (continuing). The exalted power
        Of knowledge, hidden
        From all the world,
        Is freely given   2570
        To the one who does not
        Indulge in thought.

Faust.   What kind of nonsense is she talking?
        It's giving me a splitting headache.
        I feel as if I'm listening to   2575
        The choir of an insane asylum.

Mephistopheles. Enough, enough, O wondrous sibyl!
        Give us your potion now, and fill
        The bowl right to the brim; be quick!
        This drink won't harm my friend at all: 2580
        He holds a number of degrees;
        He's swallowed a thing or two by now.

        (*The Witch, with great ceremony, pours
        the potion into a bowl. As Faust lifts it to
        his mouth a slight flame appears.*)

Mephistopheles. Just knock it back! Come on!
        You'll find it warms your heart.
        You are on intimate terms with the devil   2585
        And are intimidated by that flame?

        (*The Witch dissolves the circle. Faust steps out.*)

Mephistopheles. Outside at once! You mustn't rest.

The Witch. And may my little potion do you good!

Mephistopheles. If there's a favor you would like,
    Just tell me on Walpurgis Night.[21]   2590

The Witch. Here is a song! And if you sing it now and then,
    You'll sense astonishing effects.

Mephistopheles. Come quickly now and let me guide you;
    It's most important that you sweat,
    So that the power can penetrate.   2595
    Later you'll learn to treasure a noble life of leisure,
    And soon you'll feel, with consummate delight,
    How Cupid stirs and bounces up and down.

Faust. Let me look quickly in the mirror one more time!
    That woman's image was too beautiful!   2600

Mephistopheles. No! No! The very paradigm of women
    You'll soon see standing in the flesh before you.
    (*Softly.*) Yes, with this potion in your body, you'll soon see
    Helen in every woman you meet.

Street

    (*Faust. Margarete passing by.*)

Faust. My pretty lady, take my arm,   2605
    Allow me, please, to walk you home.

Margarete. I'm not a lady, am not pretty,
    Can walk home unaccompanied.

---

21. The night before May 1, during which the witches' sabbath was supposed to be celebrated on the Brocken. (See note to line 2113.)

(She frees herself and goes off.)

Faust.   My God, this child is beautiful!
          I've never seen the like before.   2610
          She's full of modesty and virtue,
          And yet a little saucy too.
          And those red lips and those bright cheeks,
          In all my days I won't forget them!
          The way she lowers her eyes like that,   2615
          Impressed itself deep in my heart;
          And that curt way she put me down—
          Why that is utterly enchanting!

(Mephistopheles enters.)

Faust.   Listen, you have to get that girl for me!

Mephistopheles. Which one?

Faust.   The one that just walked by.   2620

Mephistopheles. That one? She's coming from confession;
          The priest absolved her of every sin;
          I crept behind his chair to listen.
          She's an innocent little thing—
          Why, she had nothing to confess;   2625
          I have no power over her!

Faust.   But she must be at least fourteen.

Mephistopheles. You sound like Jack the Lecher,
          Who longs to have each pretty flower
          And can't imagine any honor   2630
          Or favor that's not his to pluck—
          It doesn't always work like that.

Faust.   My dear Professor Morality,
          Spare me your laws!
          And let me put it quite succinctly: 2635

Unless that sweet young thing
Is lying in my arms this evening,
You and I will part at midnight.

Mephistopheles. Be realistic please!
It will take fourteen days at least   2640
To ferret out an opportunity.

Faust. Had I but seven hours leisure,
I would not need the devil
To seduce that little creature.

Mephistopheles. You're sounding almost like a Frenchman;   2645
But please, don't get so irritated:
What good is instant gratification?
It only lessens your satisfaction;
Better to spend some time preparing
Your little dolly, softening her up   2650
With every sort of worthless bauble—
Foreign romances will teach you how.

Faust. I've appetite enough without all that.

Mephistopheles. But jokes and lectures aside,
I tell you, with that pretty child   2655
Things simply will not go so fast.
You will not capture her by storm;
Guile is the only option here.

Faust. Bring me some token from that treasured angel!
Lead me to the place she lies!   2660
Bring me a kerchief from her breast,
A garter for my love-delight!

Mephistopheles. So that you see I wish to be of use
And wish to ease your torment,
We will not waste a single moment;   2665
I'll lead you to her room this very day.

Faust.   And will I see her? Have her?

Mephistopheles.   No!
         She will be at her neighbor's house.
         Enveloped in her atmosphere,
         In solitude you'll graze your fill,   2670
         Anticipating joys to come.

Faust.   Can we go now?

Mephistopheles.   It's still too early.

Faust.   Then go find me a present for her! (*Exit.*)

Mephistopheles.   Presents? That's courteous! Then he'll succeed!
         I recollect some pretty places   2675
         And treasures buried long ago;
         This calls for some reconnaissance. (*Exit.*)

Evening

         (*A small tidy room.*)

Margarete (*braiding her hair and putting it up*).
         I would give anything to know
         Who that gentleman was today!
         He certainly looked brave and fine;   2680
         I'm sure that he's a nobleman;
         Yes, I could read it in his brow—
         And no one else would be so forward. (*Exit.*)

         (*Mephistopheles and Faust enter.*)

Mephistopheles.   Come in, but quietly, come in!

Faust (*after a pause*).   Leave me alone, I beg you!   2685

Mephistopheles (snooping around). Not every girl keeps things so
        spotless. *(Exit.)*

Faust (looking up and around). Welcome, sweet evening light, and weave
        Soft patterns through this holy place!
        Come seize my heart, sweet agonies of love
        That thirst and live on hope's fine dew!   2690
        What sense of stillness breathes about me here,
        What sense of order and contentment!
        Oh what abundance in this poverty!
        In this prison what salvation!
          (He throws himself into a leather chair by the bed.)
        Receive me too, you who with open arms   2695
        Have welcomed ages past in joy and grief!
        How often has a host of children clung
        Around this patriarchal throne!
        Here, in gratitude for the Christ Child's gifts,
        Perhaps my darling once, with round pink cheeks,   2700
        Devoutly kissed a grandfather's withered hand.
        Dear girl, I feel your spirit
        Of order and abundance wafting round me;
        Mother-like it teaches you each day,
        Tells you to spread the clean cloth smoothly on the table,   2705
        To rake the sand in ripples at your feet.
        Oh dearest hand! So godlike!
        You've turned this hut into a heavenly kingdom.
        And here! *(Lifting a bed-curtain.)* What dreadful bliss!
        Here I could while whole hours away.   2710
        Nature! Here in gentle dreams you formed
        That incarnate angel![22]
        Here lay the child, its tiny breast
        Suffused with warmth and life,
        And here, with pure and holy weaving   2715
        The image of God came into being!

        And you, Faust! What has brought you here?
        I feel myself profoundly moved!

---

22.   The word *eingeboren* means both "only-begotten" or "unique" and "inborn" or "innate."

What do you want here? Why does your heart grow heavy?
Wretched Faust, I hardly know you!   2720

Do magic fragrances surround me here?
I longed to gratify my lust
And feel myself dissolve in dreams of love!
Are we the playthings of each passing breeze?
And if she were to enter at this moment,   2725
How you'd atone then for your sacrilege!
How small the great man would be then,
Prostrate and melting at her feet.

Mephistopheles. Quickly! I see her coming down below.

Faust. Away! Away! I'm never coming here again!   2730

Mephistopheles. Here is a little box—don't worry, it's quite heavy—
I retrieved it from another place.
Just set it here, inside her cabinet;
I swear she'll lose her wits—
The trinkets I put in it would win over   2735
A girl with higher aspirations.
But then, a girl's a girl; a game's a game.

Faust. I don't know—should I?

Mephistopheles.   But why keep asking?
Do you plan to keep the treasure for yourself?
If so, I humbly advise Your Avarice   2740
Not to waste my precious time,
And to spare me further efforts.
I really hope you're not a miser!
I rack my brains, wear out my fingers—
    (*He sets the little box in the closet and closes the latch.*)
Away now, fast—   2745
To make this sweet young child
Bend to your heart's desire and will.
But you stand there and look

As if you're waiting to attend a lecture,
As if the grey-haired ladies, Physics   2750
And Metaphysics, stood before you in the flesh!
Away! (*Exit.*)

Margarete (with a lamp). It is so sultry here, so stifling,
          (*She opens the window.*)
     Though it's not all that warm outside.
     I'm feeling so—I don't know how—   2755
     I wish that Mother would come home.
     A shiver just ran through my body—
     I am a foolish, timid woman!

     (*She begins to sing as she undresses.*)
     There was a king in Thule,
     Faithful till the grave,   2760
     To whom his dying lady
     A golden goblet gave.

     He loved that goblet so,
     He drained it at each feast;
     His eyes did overflow,   2765
     Whene'er he drank from it.

     And as he neared his grave,
     He counted up his towns;
     He gave his heirs the kingdom,
     But not the cup of gold.   2770

     And at the royal banquet,
     He sat with all his knights,
     In the great hall of his fathers,
     In the castle by the sea.

     And all his revels ended,   2775
     He drank his life's last glow,
     And threw the sacred goblet
     Down in the stream below.

He watched it fall and drink,
And sink deep in the sea,   2780
His eyes began to sink—
He never drank again.

*(She opens the closet to put her clothes
away and sees the jewel box.)*
How did this pretty little box get here?
I'm sure I locked the cabinet.
That's strange! I wonder what could be inside it?   2785
Maybe someone pawned it in exchange
For money that my mother loaned him.
And there's a little key here on a ribbon—
I think I'll open it!
What *is* this? God in heaven! Look,   2790
I've never seen the like!
What gems! A noblewoman might go out
In jewels like this on special holidays.
What would this chain look like on me?
To whom can all this splendor belong?   2795
   *(She adorns herself with it and steps
   in front of the mirror.)*
If only these earrings were mine!
They make me look quite different.
What use is beauty, after all, or youth?
Oh yes, they're fine and good, no doubt,
But no one really cares about all that;   2800
Half-pitying they praise your beauty.
And in the end,
All things depend on gold,
Throng toward gold. Alas we poor!

Promenade

*(Faust, walking back and forth lost in
thought. Mephistopheles joins him.)*

Mephistopheles. By all rejected love! By the infernal element!   2805
   I wish I knew of something worse—I'd swear by it too!

Faust.   Why what's the matter now? What's biting you?
         I've never seen a face like that in all my life!

Mephistopheles. I'd like to give myself straight over to the devil—
         If I were not already one myself!   2810

Faust.   Has a screw come loose inside your head?
         It suits you, though, to play the raging madman!

Mephistopheles. Can you believe it, the jewels that I procured for
                Gretchen—
         A priest has snatched them clean away!
         Her mother takes one look at them   2815
         And starts to feel a secret dread:
         Her sense of smell has grown so subtle,
         From constant sniffing in her missal,
         That she can tell just by the scent
         Whether an article is sacred or profane.   2820
         And she could sense quite clearly
         That those jewels weren't altogether holy.
         "Dear child," she cried, "treasures of wickedness[23]
         Ensnare the soul, devour the blood.
         We'll give these riches to God's Mother,   2825
         And she'll reward us with heavenly manna!"
         Then little Margaret began to pout;
         Why look a gift horse in the mouth, she thought,
         And after all, the man who brought this
         So gallantly cannot be godless!   2830
         Her mother had a priest come over;
         He soon took in the fun
         And savored the delicious sight.
         He said, "That is the proper spirit:
         Who overcomes[24] shall triumph in the end.   2835
         The church has a hearty appetite
         And has consumed entire nations
         Without a hint of indigestion;

23. See Proverbs 10:2.
24. See Revelation 2:17.

       The church alone, dear ladies, can
       Assimilate ill-gotten gains."   2840

Faust.   But kings and Jews can swallow them too—
       The practice is widespread.[25]

Mephistopheles. And then he swiped a brooch, a chain, a ring,
       As if they were mere crumbs,
       With no more gratitude   2845
       Than if you'd given him a bag of nuts;
       He promised them rewards in heaven—
       They must have been most edified.

Faust.   And Gretchen?

Mephistopheles.   Sits restlessly,
       Not knowing what she wants or ought to do;   2850
       She thinks about the jewelry day and night,
       And of the man who brought it to her.

Faust.   My darling's sorrow saddens me;
       Go get new jewelry for her right away!
       The first was really nothing much, you know.   2855

Mephistopheles. Oh yes, to you it's all child's play!

Faust.   Hurry, arrange things as I want!
       Go get acquainted with her neighbor!
       Quickly, devil—don't drag your feet—
       Go get new jewels and bring them here!   2860

Mephistopheles. Indeed, my gracious lord, with pleasure.

      (Exit Faust.)

---

25.   Only Jews and the magistrate himself were exempt from the prohibition against usury.

Mephistopheles. A fool in love will send the sun,
    The moon, and all the stars up in a puff
    Of smoke—pinwheels to amuse his sweetheart. (*Exit.*)

The Neighbor's House

Martha (alone). God forgive my dear husband,   2865
    He's not done well by me at all!
    Goes out into the world to fight
    And leaves me here alone in my straw bed.
    I really didn't cause much trouble,
    Loved him, God knows, with all my heart.   2870
      (*She weeps.*)
    He may be dead for all I know!
    If only I'd a death-certificate!

    (*Margarete enters.*)

Margarete. Martha!

Martha.   What is it, Gretchen dear?

Margarete. My legs are shaking—I can barely stand!
    I found another little box   2875
    Inside my cabinet—made of ebony—
    And really glorious things in it,
    And far more precious than before.

Martha. You mustn't tell your mother;
    She'd take it to the priest again.   2880

Margarete. Oh, just see this! Just look at this!

Martha (putting a necklace on Gretchen). You lucky creature!

Margarete. I mustn't let myself be seen
    Out on the street or in church with it.

Martha. Come visit me as often as you like   2885
        And try the jewels on secretly;
        Walk back and forth a while before the mirror here,
        And we'll enjoy them privately;
        On some occasion then, a holiday,
        You'll gradually begin to let some people see them.   2890
        A small chain first, and then a pearl in your ear—
        Your mother will not see, or we'll invent some story.

Margarete. Who could have brought these boxes to me?
        There's something not quite right about it!
            (*A knock at the door.*)
        Oh God! Is that my mother?   2895

Martha (*looking through the peephole*). A foreign gentleman—come in!

            (*Mephistopheles enters.*)

Mephistopheles. I took the liberty of coming unannounced;
        Most humbly beg forgiveness, ladies.
            (*Steps back courteously from Margarete.*)
        I'm looking for Frau Martha Schwerdtlein!

Martha. That's me, what have you got to say, sir?   2900

Mephistopheles (*in a low voice*). We are acquainted, that's enough for
                now;
        I see you have distinguished company.
        So please, excuse the liberty I took;
        I'll come again this afternoon.

Martha (*aloud*). Imagine, child, of all things in the world!   2905
        This gentleman thinks you're a lady.

Margarete. I'm young and poor, and have no noble blood;
        Oh Lord, sir, you are far too good:
        These jewels and gemstones are not mine.

Mephistopheles. Oh it is not the jewels alone;   2910
    You have such presence, such penetrating eyes!
    I'm just delighted I may stay!

Martha. What have you brought? I really want—

Mephistopheles. I wish I had some happier news!
    I hope you won't make me regret it: 2915
    Your husband's dead and sends his greetings.

Martha. He's dead? That faithful heart! Oh!
    My husband's dead! I think I'll die!

Margarete. Dear Martha! Don't despair!

Mephistopheles. Come, listen to the tragic tale!   2920

Margarete. I'd rather never fall in love;
    I'd die of grief at such a loss.

Mephistopheles. Sorrow and joy always go hand in hand.

Martha. Tell me about his life's sad end!

Mephistopheles. He's lying in a grave in Padua,   2925
    Right by St. Anthony's basilica,
    In ground that's been well-blessed,
    A cool, eternal bed of rest.

Martha. But have you brought me nothing else?

Mephistopheles. Yes, one request—I fear it's onerous—   2930
    He'd like three hundred masses said for him!
    Apart from that my pocket's empty.

Martha. What! Not a single jewel? No medal?
    The sort of keepsake every poor apprentice

Hides at the very bottom of his bag,   2935
Because he'd rather starve than part with it?

Mephistopheles. You have my deepest sympathy,
But really, ma'am, he did not squander money.
He showed remorse for his mistakes,
Yes, and lamented his misfortunes even more.   2940

Margarete. Oh, why are people so unfortunate!
I'll certainly say some requiems for him.

Mephistopheles. You deserve to find a husband right away:
You are an amiable child.

Margarete. Oh no, it's far too soon for that.   2945

Mephistopheles. If not a husband, then, a lover.
It's one of heaven's greatest blessings
To hold a darling thing like you in one's arms.

Margarete. That's not the practice in this country.

Mephistopheles. Practice or not, it happens occasionally.   2950

Martha. Tell me the story!

Mephistopheles.   I was standing at his deathbed—
It wasn't much better than a dung heap,
The straw half-rotten—yet he died a Christian
And found he'd far more debts than he could pay.
He cried, "How I detest myself to the core,   2955
Abandoning my trade, my wife, like that!
It kills me to remember it—
I do wish she'd forgive me before I die!"

Martha (weeping). The good man! I forgave him long ago.

Mephistopheles. "Although, God knows, she's more to blame
        than me."   2960

Martha. What! That's a lie! On the brink of his grave and telling lies!

Mephistopheles. I'm sure he told some feverish tales as he lay dying;
    I'm quite a connoisseur in these affairs.
    "I had," he said, "no time to spare,
    First children, and then getting bread for them—   2965
    I mean bread in the widest sense—
    Then too, I couldn't even eat my share in peace."

Martha. Did he forget all my devotion, all my love,
    The way I slaved both day and night?

Mephistopheles. Oh by no means, he thought of you with
        great affection.   2970
    He said, "When I set sail from Malta,
    How ardently I prayed for my wife and children;
    Then heaven smiled auspiciously on us;
    Our ship soon took a Turkish vessel
    Bearing the mighty Sultan's treasure.   2975
    Then courage was rewarded,
    And I received, as was my due,
    A fair share of the spoils."

Martha. How's that? And where? Perhaps he buried it?

Mephistopheles. Who knows where the four winds have
        scattered it.   2980
    A pretty lady took him in—
    He was a stranger in the streets of Naples;
    She was so loving, so devoted,
    He felt it till his dying day.[26]

---

26. Syphilis was known as *le mal de Naples* or *le mal napolitain*.

Martha. The scoundrel! Stealing from his children!   2985
    Not even need and misery
    Could turn him from a life of shame!

Mephistopheles. But see, he's dead now, isn't he?
    If I were in your shoes right now,
    I'd mourn him for a decent year;   2990
    Meanwhile I'd set my sights on some new treasure.

Martha. Oh Lord! Where in the world will I ever find
    Another like my first!
    There's never been a more affectionate fool.
    His only fault was love of travel,   2995
    And foreign women and foreign wine,
    And that damned game of dice.

Mephistopheles. Well, that would be alright,
    If he, for his part, had been willing
    To overlook as many faults in you.   3000
    I swear, on terms like that, I'd be prepared
    To exchange a ring with you myself!

Martha. You gentlemen will have your jokes!

Mephistopheles (to himself). I'd best clear out of here and fast!
    She'd hold the very devil to his word.   3005
    (To Gretchen.) And what about your heart?

Margarete. What do you mean, sir?

Mephistopheles (to himself).   You good and innocent child!
    (Aloud.) Ladies, farewell!

Margarete.   Farewell!

Martha.   But tell me quickly!
    I'd like to have some evidence,

Where, how, and when my treasure died, was buried.   3010
I've always liked to keep things tidy;
I'd like to read in the paper that he's dead.

Mephistopheles. Good woman, yes of course. The testimony
Of two witnesses is always true.
I have an excellent companion;   3015
I'll have him go before the judge on your behalf.
Let me go get him.

Martha.   Oh yes, please do!

Mephistopheles. Will this young lady be there too?
He's a fine fellow, widely traveled,
And always courteous to young ladies.   3020

Margarete. I'd turn beet-red in front of such a man.

Mephistopheles. And were he king, you'd have no cause to blush.

Martha. Behind the house, there in my garden
We will expect you gentlemen this evening.

Street

(*Faust and Mephistopheles.*)

Faust.   How is it going? Will it work? And soon?   3025

Mephistopheles. Bravo! Do I find you on fire?
In no time Gretchen will be yours;
Tonight you'll see her at her neighbor Martha's house:
Now there's a woman who's cut out
For pandering and gypsy work!   3030

Faust.   Splendid!

Mephistopheles.   But something is required of us as well.

Faust.   One good turn deserves another.

Mephistopheles. We have to act as witnesses and testify:
        Her husband's limbs lie stretched out peacefully
        And rest in consecrated ground in Padua.   3035

Faust.   How very clever! Now we have to take a trip!

Mephistopheles. Holy Simplicity! No need for that;
        Just testify, without much knowledge.

Faust.   If that's the best that you can do, forget the plan.

Mephistopheles. O holy man! That's you all over!   3040
        Is this the first time in your life
        That you have borne false witness?
        Didn't you, bold-faced and confident,
        Once give authoritative definitions
        Of God, and of the world and all that moves in it,   3045
        Of man and all that stirs within his head and heart?
        And if you think it over properly,
        You must admit, you knew as much about those things
        As you do now about Herr Schwerdtlein's death!

Faust.   You are and will remain a liar and a sophist.   3050

Mephistopheles. True, if I did not know a little more.
        Will you not very soon and in all honor
        Befool poor Gretchen, yes, and swear
        That you love her with all your soul?

Faust.   Why yes, wholeheartedly!

Mephistopheles.   That's excellent!   3055
        Then you'll speak of eternal fidelity and love,

And of a single drive that overpowers all else[27]—
Will that then be wholehearted too?

Faust.   Stop that! It will be! When I feel
And try in vain to find a name   3060
For this feeling, this turmoil,
And cast my thoughts about the world,
Grasp at all the most exalted words,
And call the ardor that inflames me
Endless—eternal—yes, eternal,   3065
Is that a devilish game of deceit?

Mephistopheles. You'll find I'm right!

Faust.   Take note of this,
I beg you—spare my lungs—
Whoever wants to prove he's right and has a tongue
Will certainly prove right.   3070
Now come, I'm tired of chit-chat.
Yes, you are right—mainly because I have no choice.

Garden

(Margarete on Faust's arm. Martha strolling
back and forth with Mephistopheles.)

Margarete. I feel it, sir, you're trying to spare me,
Lowering yourself—and I'm ashamed.
A traveler's used to that   3075
And puts up graciously with what he finds;
I know too well that my poor talk
Can't entertain a man of your experience.

27.   The adjective *überallmächtig* or "over-all-potent," which occurs only here, can mean either "having power over all things" or "powerful everywhere." It can also mean "more than omnipotent."

Faust.   One glance from you, one word, will entertain
             Me more than all the wisdom of this world.   3080
                  (*He kisses her hand.*)

Margarete. Oh don't demean yourself like that! How can you kiss it?
             It's awfully coarse and rough!
             What haven't I already had to do!
             My mother's very hard to please.
                  (*They pass by.*)

Martha. And you, sir, do you always travel like this?   3085

Mephistopheles. Business and duty drive me to it, I'm afraid!
             How sad I am to leave some places,
             And yet I simply cannot stay!

Martha. It's fine to breeze about the world
             While you're still young and active,   3090
             But then, when bad times come along,
             To drag yourself, alone, a bachelor, to the grave,
             That surely can't be pleasant.

Mephistopheles. I'm filled with horror at the prospect.

Martha. Then worthy sir, take my advice while there's still time.   3095
                  (*They pass by.*)

Margarete. Yes, out of sight, out of mind!
             You're fluent in these courteous manners,
             But you have heaps of friends;
             I know they're cleverer than me.

Faust.   Best one! Believe me, what's called clever   3100
             Is often narrow-minded vanity.

Margarete.   How's that?

Faust.   Oh that simplicity and innocence
             Can never know themselves, their holy worth!

Humility and lowliness, the highest gifts
That nature lovingly apportions— 3105

Margarete. If you will think of me just for a moment,
I will have time enough to think of you.

Faust. I suppose you're frequently alone?

Margarete. Oh yes, our household is quite small,
And still it must be tended to. 3110
We have no maid; I have to cook and sweep, to knit
And sew, run errands dawn to dusk;
My mother's so exacting
About every little thing!
Not that she needs to be so frugal; 3115
We could afford to spend more than some others:
My father left a pretty legacy,
A little house and garden outside town.
But now my days are pretty quiet:
My brother is a soldier; 3120
My little sister's dead.
I had my hands full with that child, it's true,
But I'd be glad to take on all that care once more,
I loved her so.

Faust. An angel, if she was like you.

Margarete. I raised her, and she loved me dearly. 3125
She was born soon after father died.
We'd given mother up for lost,
She lay there in such misery,
And she recovered very slowly, bit by bit.
Of course she couldn't even think 3130
Of nursing the poor little mite,
And so I raised the baby on my own,
With milk and water; she was mine.
Yes, in my arms and on my lap
She smiled and wriggled and grew bigger. 3135

Faust.   I'm sure you felt the purest pleasure.

Margarete.   Hard hours as well, to be sure.
            At night the little one's cradle stood
            Right by my bed; she'd barely stir,
            And I'd wake up;   3140
            I'd give her a drink, lay her beside me,
            Then if she didn't settle, I'd get up
            And rock her as I walked her up and down the room;
            And early in the day I'd do the wash,
            Then go to market, then stand at the stove,   3145
            Day in, day out the same.
            Then, sir, it's hard to keep your spirits up,
            But in return you relish food and rest.
               (*They pass by.*)

Martha.   We women are unfortunate:
            A bachelor's not easy to convert.   3150

Mephistopheles.   It would just take someone like you
            To teach me a better way of life.

Martha.   Tell me the truth, have you found nothing, sir,
            Was there no place your heart became attached?

Mephistopheles.   A hearth of one's own, a virtuous wife,   3155
            The proverb says, are worth as much as gold and pearls.[28]

Martha.   I mean, haven't you ever felt the desire?

Mephistopheles.   I've been received politely everywhere.

Martha.   I'm asking whether you have ever loved in earnest.

Mephistopheles.   With ladies one should never undertake to jest.   3160

---

28.   The proverb in fact claims that a virtuous woman is to be prized "far above rubies" (AKJV), or "is more noble than the most precious pearls" (in Luther's German translation). See Proverbs 31:10.

Martha. Oh you don't understand!

Mephistopheles.   I'm very sorry!
 Although I understand—that you're extremely gracious.
  (*They pass by.*)

Faust. You recognized me, little angel, then,
 As soon as I came in the garden?

Margarete. Couldn't you tell? I lowered my eyes.   3165

Faust. And you forgive the liberty I took?
 The impudent way I spoke,
 As you came out of church that day?

Margarete. I was upset, that never happened to me before;
 No one could say bad things about me.   3170
 Did he, I wondered, see in your behavior
 Something impudent, improper?
 He simply seemed to think I was a girl
 He could be very forward with.
 And I admit I did not know what then   3175
 Began to stir in me and take your part;
 I really was quite angry with myself
 That I could not be angrier with you.

Faust. Sweet darling!

Margarete.   Let me finish!
 (*She picks a daisy and plucks the petals off, one by one.*)

Faust.   What's that? A bouquet?

Margarete. No, just a game.

Faust.   What?

Margarete.   Go! You'll laugh at me.   3180

(She plucks and murmurs.)

Faust.   What are you murmuring?

Margarete (softly).   He loves me—loves me not.

Faust.   You gentle face of heaven!

Margarete (continuing). Loves me—not—loves me—not—
        (Pulling out the last petal, with gentle joy.)
        He loves me!

Faust.   Yes, my child! This flower-word
        Shall be a prophecy to you. He loves you!   3185
        Do you understand what that means? He loves you!
        (He takes her hands.)

Margarete. I'm trembling!

Faust.   Oh do not shudder! Let my eyes,
        The touch of my hand tell you
        What no voice can express: 3190
        To give oneself completely and to feel
        A bliss that must be eternal!
        Eternal! Its end would be despair.
        No! No end! No end!

        *(Margarete clasps his hands, then frees
        herself and runs off. He stands lost in thought
        for a moment and then follows her.)*

Martha (entering). Night is falling.

Mephistopheles.   Yes, and we must go.   3195

Martha. I would ask you to stay a little longer,
        But this is a bad, bad place.
        It's as if they'd nothing at all to do,
        No occupation,

But to gape at every step their neighbor takes;   3200
They'll gossip about you, no matter what you do.
And our little pair?

Mephistopheles.   Has flown along that path.
     Light-hearted butterflies!

Martha.   He's partial to her.

Mephistopheles. And she to him. And so the world follows its course.

A Small Garden-House

> (*Margarete dashes inside, hides behind the door, puts
> her forefinger to her lips, and peeks through the crack.*)

Margarete. He's coming!

Faust (entering).   Little rascal, teasing me like this!   3205
     Now I've caught you! (*Kisses her.*)

Margarete (embracing him and returning his kiss).
          Best of men! With all my heart I love you!

> (*Mephistopheles knocks.*)

Faust (stamping his foot). Who's there?

Mephistopheles.   A friend!

Faust.   A beast!

Mephistopheles.   It's time for us to leave.

Martha (entering). It's getting late, sir.

Faust.   May I not walk you home?

Margarete. My mother would—goodbye!

Faust.   Then do I have to go?
         Farewell!

Martha.   Goodbye!

Margarete.   Until we meet again!   3210

         (Faust and Mephistopheles leave.)

Margarete. Dear God! How many, many things
         A man like that can think about!
         I feel ashamed when I am with him,
         And just say yes to everything.
         I'm such a poor uneducated child,   3215
         I can't think what he sees in me.   *(Exit.)*

Forest and Cave

Faust (alone). Sublime spirit, you gave me, gave me all
         I asked. Not for nothing did you turn
         Your countenance toward me in the fire.
         You gave me glorious nature as my kingdom,   3220
         The power to feel it, to enjoy it. Not only
         Cold admiring visits did you grant me;
         You let me gaze deep into nature's breast,
         As if into the heart of some dear friend.
         You lead the ranks of living beings by me   3225
         And teach me how to recognize my brothers
         In quiet groves and in the air and water.
         And when the storm roars, crashing through the forest,
         And the giant spruce tree, falling, knocks down neighboring
         Branches and trunks, and at the blow the hillside   3230
         Reverberates with dull and hollow thunder,
         Then you lead me to a sheltered cave
         And show me my own self, and secret wonders
         Deep inside my breast disclose themselves.

And when before my eyes the pure moon rises,   3235
Spreading its soothing light, then from the cliff-face
And from dew-laden bushes, silvery forms
Of ages past float slowly up toward me
And ease the stern delight of contemplation.

Humanity is granted nothing perfect—   3240
I see that now. For with this bliss that brings me
Close and closer to the gods, you gave me
The associate I cannot do without,
Though cold and insolent he lowers me
In my own eyes, reducing all your gifts   3245
To nothing with his subtle whispers.
Relentlessly he fans within my breast
Wild flames of longing for that lovely image.
I stagger from desire to enjoyment,
And in enjoyment thirst for that desire.   3250

    (*Mephistopheles enters*).

Mephistopheles. Haven't you had enough of this life yet?
How can it satisfy you in the long run?
No doubt it's fine to try it out,
But then move on to something new!

Faust. I wish you'd something else to do,   3255
Than to torment me on a good day.

Mephistopheles. Well, well! I'm glad to let you rest;
No need to get annoyed about it.
Such a companion—surly, rude, insane—
It really would be no great loss.   3260
One has one's hands full all day long!
What pleases him and what's forbidden
Is hard to sense from the gentleman's expression.

Faust. That's just your customary tone!
Am I to thank you, then, for irritating me?   3265

Mephistopheles. And how would you, poor son of earth,
      Have led your life without me?
      I cured you for a while at least
      Of your deranged imaginings.
      And were it not for me, you would have stepped   3270
      Right off this earthly globe by now.
      Why do you sit hunched like an owl
      In caverns and in crevices?
      Why do you, like a toad, suck nourishment
      From sodden moss and dripping rocks?   3275
      A sweet and lovely way to pass the time!
      At heart you're still the old professor.

Faust.   Do you not see what new vitality
      This sojourn in the wilderness affords me?
      Had you the least suspicion of it,   3280
      You'd be devil enough to grudge me this joy.

Mephistopheles. Truly, an unearthly pleasure!
      To lie upon the hills in night and dew,
      Embracing earth and heaven with rapture,
      To swell up to a godly size,   3285
      To pierce earth's marrow with prescient urges,
      To feel all six days' work deep in your breast,
      Proudly enjoying who knows what,
      To overflow in ecstasies of love,
      A son of earth no longer,   3290
      And then your lofty intuition—
        (Makes an obscene gesture.)
      I won't say how—concludes the act.

Faust.   Shame on you!

Mephistopheles.   You are offended;
      You have the right politely to say, "Shame!"
      Chaste ears refuse to let one mention   3295
      What chaste hearts can't refrain from.
      In short, I don't grudge you the pleasure—
      Delude yourself from time to time—

But you will not hold out for long.
Already you are driven onward, 3300
And if it takes much longer, you will be reduced
To madness, or to fear and horror!
Enough of that! Your darling sits indoors
And finds her world constricted, gloomy.
She can't get you out of her head; 3305
She's overwhelmed with love for you.
First, like a little stream that overspills its banks
When the snow melts in the spring, your overflowing,
Furious passion flooded her heart;
Now your small stream runs dry again. 3310
I think, instead of ruling forests,
It would become the great lord better
To compensate that poor young monkey
For all her love.
She finds the time intolerably slow; 3315
She stands at the window, watches the clouds pass by
Over the ancient city-wall.
"Were I a little bird," so goes her song,[29]
All the day long, half the night long.
At times she's cheerful, but mostly troubled; 3320
At times she cries until her tears run dry;
Then she's quiet again, or so it seems,
And always she's in love.

Faust.   Serpent! Serpent!

Mephistopheles (to himself). Yes, let me catch you! 3325

Faust.   Away from here, you reprobate!
And do not mention that beautiful woman!
Don't make me lust for her sweet body—
My senses are half-crazed already!

Mephistopheles. What do you want? She thinks you've left her, 3330
And really, more or less, you have.

29. A German folk song.

Faust.   I'm near to her, and were I yet so far,
           I can't forget her, cannot cast her off;
           Yes, I am even jealous of Christ's body,
           Each time her lips reach out to take the host.   3335

Mephistopheles. That's it, my friend! I've often envied you
           Those twin young roes, which feed among the lilies.[30]

Faust.   Panderer, leave!

Mephistopheles.   Oh scold away—it makes me laugh.
           The god who first created boys and girls
           Pursued this noble calling too—   3340
           Provided them with ways to multiply.
           Now go, this is pathetic!
           You're heading to your darling's bedroom,
           Not to your death.

Faust.   What is the joy of heaven in her arms?   3345
           Yes, let me warm myself upon her breast!
           Do I not still feel all her anguish?
           Am I not fugitive? Unhoused?
           Inhuman without aim or rest,
           Roaring like a waterfall from cliff to cliff,   3350
           In greedy rage toward the abyss?
           Off to the side with dim and childlike thoughts,
           She in her hut upon the little alpine meadow,
           All her domestic doings
           Enclosed within that little world.[31]   3355
           And I, the god-detested,
           Was not satisfied
           To grasp the cliffs
           And shatter them!
           Her, her peace, I had to undermine!   3360
           You, Hell, required this sacrifice!

---

30.   Song of Solomon 4:5.

31.   The breakdown in syntax is Faust's.

Help, devil, help me shorten the time of fear!
What must come, let it come at once!
On me, then, may her doom crash down,
And she, in turn, go under with me! 3365

Mephistopheles. How you're seething, how you're glowing!
Go in, you fool! Console her!
Where little minds can't find an exit,
They instantly imagine a disaster.
Well here's to steadfast men! 3370
In most respects you're fairly well bedeviled.
There's nothing in the world I find more tasteless,
Than a devil who despairs.

Gretchen's Room

(Gretchen at the spinning wheel, alone.)

My quiet is gone,
My heart is heavy; 3375
I'll never find
My quiet again.

When he's not here,
All seems a grave
And all the world 3380
Is filled with gall.

And my poor head
Begins to reel,
And my poor wits
Are torn apart. 3385

My quiet is gone,
My heart is heavy;
I'll never find
My quiet again.

For him alone   3390
I look out the window,
For him alone
I go out the door.

His gracious bearing,
His noble form,   3395
The smile on his lips,
The force of his eyes,

And the magical flow
Of his voice, and then,
The touch of his hand,   3400
And oh his kiss!

My quiet is gone,
My heart is heavy;
I'll never find
My quiet again.   3405

And I so long
To be with him.
Oh could I only have
And hold him,

And kiss him then   3410
The way I wish—
Pass away
In his kiss!

Martha's Garden

> (*Margarete and Faust.*)

Margarete. Promise me, Heinrich!

Faust.   Anything I can!

Margarete.   Then tell me how you feel about religion.   3415
        You are a good man, heart and soul,
        But I believe you don't think much of it.

Faust.   Leave that, my child! You sense that I am fond of you;
        For those I love I'd give my body and my blood;
        There's no one I'd deny his feeling and his church.   3420

Margarete.   That isn't right, one must believe in it!

Faust.   Must one?

Margarete.   I wish I had some influence on you!
        You don't respect the holy sacraments.

Faust.   I do respect them.

Margarete.   But you don't desire them.
        It's ages since you've been to mass or to confession.   3425
        Do you believe in God?

Faust.   My darling, who can say:
        I believe in God?
        Ask men of learning, ask the priests—
        Their answer simply seems
        To mock the one who's asking.

Margarete.   Then you don't believe?   3430

Faust.   O gentle face, do not misunderstand me!
        Who can name him?
        Who can confess:
        I believe in him?
        Who that has feeling   3435
        Can ever undertake
        To say: I don't believe in him?
        All-embracing,

All-sustaining,
Does he not embrace and sustain   3440
You, me, himself?
Does not the sky arch high above?
Does not the earth lie firm below?
And do eternal stars not rise,
Glancing kindly down on us?   3445
Do I not look into your eyes,
And do not all things surge and throng
Toward your head and heart,
And weave, in their eternal mystery,
Invisibly and visibly beside you?   3450
Then fill your heart with this, great as it is,
And when you're full of rapture at the feeling,
Then call it what you will,
Call it happiness! Heart! Love! God!
I have no name   3455
For it! Feeling is all;
Names are but sound and smoke,
Clouding heaven's light.

Margarete. Well that's alright;
   The priest says more or less the same,   3460
   Except in slightly different words.

Faust. Everywhere under heaven's sun,
   All hearts say it,
   Each in his own tongue;
   Shall I not say it, then, in mine?   3465

Margarete. And put like that, it might seem fine,
   But something must be twisted in it:
   You haven't got the Christian faith.

Faust. Dear child!

Margarete.　　　　　It's bothered me for quite a while
   To see you in such company.   3470

Faust.   But why?

Margarete.   The person that you have with you,
           My inmost soul detests him so,
           And nothing in my life has ever
           Given my heart so sharp a sting
           As his repulsive face.   3475

Faust.   Sweet puppet, do not be afraid of him!

Margarete. His presence makes my blood run cold.
           I have no other enemies;
           But no matter how much I long to see you,
           I've an uncanny dread of that man,   3480
           And think he's a real rascal too!
           May God forgive me, if I'm wrong!

Faust.   The world must have its strange birds too.

Margarete. I wouldn't want to live with such a person!
           Whenever he comes in the door,   3485
           He looks around with such disdain,
           Almost ferociously;
           He has no sympathy for anything
           And doesn't love a single soul—
           It's written clearly on his brow.   3490
           I feel so happy in your arms,
           So free, so irresistibly warm;
           His presence ties me up in knots inside.

Faust.   You prescient angel!

Margarete. It overpowers me so strongly,   3495
           And every time I see him coming,
           I think that I don't love you anymore.
           When he's around, I cannot pray,
           And that's what's eating at my heart;
           You, Heinrich, you must feel it too.   3500

Faust.   Perhaps it's just bad chemistry.

Margarete.   I have to go now.

Faust.   Oh can I never spend one hour,
      Resting calmly on your breast,
      Pressing heart to heart and soul to soul?

Margarete.   Oh if I only slept alone!   3505
      I'd gladly leave the latch undone for you tonight;
      But Mother never has slept deeply,
      And if she caught us,
      She'd kill me on the spot!

Faust.   My angel, there's no need for that.   3510
      Here's a small vial! Just three drops
      In her drink and she'll soon be
      Cocooned in deep and soothing sleep.

Margarete.   What will I not do for your sake?
      I hope it will not do her any harm!   3515

Faust.   Darling, would I suggest it, if it could?

Margarete.   If I but look at you, dear man,
      Something moves me, according to your will;
      I've done so much for you already,
      There's almost nothing left for me to do. *(Exit.)*   3520

      (Mephistopheles enters.)

Mephistopheles.   The little monkey! Is she gone?

Faust.   Still spying, are you?

Mephistopheles.   I heard exactly what was happening;
      The Doctor was severely catechized;

I hope you're all the better for it.
These girls do like to find out if one's pious 3525
And observes the ancient rites; if he bows
His head in church, they think, he'll bow to my will too.

Faust. You fiend, you do not see
How this devoted, loving soul,
Full of the faith 3530
That alone
Brings her salvation, is enduring holy torments,
Afraid the man she loves so dearly may be lost.

Mephistopheles. You supersensual sensual suitor,
A little girl has led you by the nose. 3535

Faust. You grotesque progeny of mud and fire!

Mephistopheles. And she has mastered physiognomy
And in my presence feels—she can't say what!
My little mask reveals a hidden meaning;
She senses that I'm certainly a genius, 3540
Perhaps a devil even.
Well, and tonight—?

Faust. And what has that to do with you?

Mephistopheles. Well, I derive some pleasure from it too!

At the Well

(*Gretchen and Lieschen with jugs.*)

Lieschen. Have you heard about little Barbara?

Gretchen. No, not a word. I don't get out much. 3545

Lieschen. It's true, Sibyl told me so today!
    She's gone and made a fool of herself.
    And she was such a snob!

Gretchen.   What's that?

Lieschen.   It stinks!
    She's feeding two now when she eats and drinks.

Gretchen. Oh!   3550

Lieschen. It serves her right.
    She clung to him so long!
    All that walking out,
    That taking her to town, to every dance,
    Always insisting she go first;   3555
    He courted her with pastries and with wine;
    She fancied she was quite a beauty,
    But was so brazen, she was not ashamed
    To take the gifts he gave her.
    The way they kissed and licked—   3560
    Well now that little flower's picked!

Gretchen. Poor thing!

Lieschen.   Don't tell me you feel sorry for her!
    While the likes of us were busy spinning,
    And our mothers made us stay indoors in the evening,
    She was out there with her sweetheart;   3565
    On the bench by the door and in dark passageways,
    They never found the hours too long.
    So let her bow her head down now and kneel
    By the door of the church in a sinner's shirt![32]

Gretchen. Surely he'll marry her.   3570

---

32. The legally prescribed humiliation of an unwed mother; it was not abolished in Weimar, despite Goethe's own efforts, until 1786.

Lieschen. He'd be a simpleton! An agile fellow
    Will find fresh air some other place.
    And anyway, he's gone.

Gretchen.   That isn't nice at all!

Lieschen. If she gets him, we'll make her suffer.
    The boys will tear her bridal wreath apart,   3575
    And we'll scatter straw at her door.

Gretchen (walking home). Before, how boldly I'd belittle
    Some poor girl who'd gone astray!
    How I'd condemn the sins of others—
    My tongue could not find words enough!   3580
    Black as it seemed, I made it blacker;
    I couldn't make it black enough,
    And blessed myself and acted big,
    And now I've bared myself to sin!
    But—everything that drove me to it,   3585
    God! Was so good! Oh was so dear!

By the City Wall

    *(In a niche in the wall, a statue of the Mater
    Dolorosa, with vases of flowers in front of it.)*

Gretchen (putting fresh flowers in the vases).
    Incline,
    O lady of sorrows, turn
    Your face in mercy to my need!

    With a sword in your heart,[33]   3590
    With countless sorrows,
    You lift your eyes to your Son's death.

---

33. Cf. the medieval Latin hymn *Stabat mater dolorosa* ("The sorrowing mother stood"), especially the second stanza: *Cuius animam gementem / contristatam et dolentem / pertransivit gladius* ("Whose weeping soul, / compassionate and sorrowful, / a sword has pierced").

You lift your eyes to the Father,
And send your sighs above,
Sighs for His and your sad need.   3595

Who can feel
How this sorrow
Burrows through my bones?
How my poor, poor heart is trembling,
How it's shivering, how it's pining,   3600
No one knows but you alone!

No matter where I go,
It aches, it aches, aches so
Here inside my breast.
As soon as I'm alone,   3605
I weep, I weep, weep so,
The heart within me breaks.

The pots outside my window
I watered with tears, alas,
Early this morning as   3610
I broke these flowers for you.

And when the bright sun rose
And burst into my room,
I was already sitting up
In all my misery.   3615

Help! Save me from disgrace and death!
Incline,
O lady of sorrows, turn
Your face in mercy to my need!

Night

(A street in front of Gretchen's door.)

Valentin (a soldier, Gretchen's brother).

It used to be when I'd sit there drinking	3620
And other fellows would be boasting	
Loudly in praise of girls in their prime,	
Each swearing his was the finest flower,	
Washing his words down with a drink—	
I would just sit there safe and quiet,	3625
My elbows resting on the table;	
I'd listen to all that swaggering racket,	
And stroke my beard and smile at them,	
And fill my glass and raise it high,	
And then I'd say, "To each his own!	3630
But is there any girl in the land,	
Who's equal to my dear old Gretel,	
Who can hold a candle to my sister?"	
"You can bet on that!" The cups would clang;	
Others would shout: "He's right, you know!	3635
She is the ornament of her sex!"	
Then all the braggarts would fall silent.	
And now! It makes me want to tear	
My hair and climb right up the walls!	
With needling words, with wrinkled noses,	3640
I have to hear those cowards insult me!	
I have to sit like some bad debtor	
And cringe at each chance word they say!	
I want to smash their heads together,	
But cannot even call them liars.	3645

And who comes here? What's creeping past?	
Why, if I'm right, there's two of them.	
If it's him, I'll have his hide,	
He will not leave this place alive!	

(Faust and Mephistopheles enter.)

Faust.	Over there, in the chancel window,	3650
	See how the sanctuary lamp flares upward	

And glimmers faintly and more faintly sideways,
And darkness presses in all round!
So night is falling in my breast.

Mephistopheles. And me, I'm like a lovesick cat   3655
That creeps along the fire-ladders,
Then slinks round corners silently;
I feel quite virtuous about it—
A bit of thievery, a bit of copulation.
The glorious Walpurgis Night[34]   3660
Begins to haunt my very limbs.
In just two days it will be here,
Then you'll know why you stayed awake!

Faust. And meanwhile is the treasure surfacing,
The one that's shimmering back there?   3665

Mephistopheles. You'll soon experience the pleasure,
Of unearthing that little pot of treasure.
I took a peek the other day,
Spied glorious lion-coins inside.

Faust. But not one jewel, one ring,   3670
To ornament my lady love?

Mephistopheles. I did see something like that there,
Like strings of pearls, they seemed to me.

Faust. That's what I like! I find it painful
To go to her without a gift.   3675

Mephistopheles. It really shouldn't bother you
To enjoy a thing or two for free.
Now, while the sky's aglow with stars,
You'll hear a proper work of art:

---

34. See note to line 2590.

I'll serenade her with a moral song,   3680
All the better to delude her.

    (*He sings, playing the zither.*)
Why are you here
At your darling's door,
O Kate my dear,
In the early light of day?   3685
Oh do not stay!
He'll let you in,
In the maid that out a maid
Never departed more.[35]

Oh do beware!   3690
For when it's done,
Why then he's gone,
You poor, poor things!
Oh do take care,
And do no thief   3695
Any kind of favor,
Before you've a ring on your finger.

Valentin (*stepping forward*). Who are you seducing there?
    Damned rat-catcher![36]
    To the devil with your instrument!   3700
    To the devil with the singer too!

Mephistopheles. My zither's split in two! It's no use any more.

Valentin. And now let's split some skulls!

Mephistopheles (*to Faust*). Doctor, don't yield! Look lively!
    Keep close, I'll guide you.   3705

---

35.   See Ophelia's song, "Tomorrow is Saint Valentine's day," in Shakespeare's *Hamlet* (*Hamlet*, 4.5, lines 48–55).

36.   In Shakespeare's *Romeo and Juliet*, Mercutio challenges Tybalt with the words, "Tybalt, you rat-catcher, will you walk?" (*Romeo and Juliet*, 3.1, line 75).

Get out your feather duster!³⁷
Now thrust! I'll parry.

Valentin. Parry that!

Mephistopheles.   Why not?

Valentin. And this!

Mephistopheles.   Of course!

Valentin.   I think the devil's fencing here!
  What's this? My hand has suddenly gone numb.   3710

Mephistopheles (to Faust). Thrust!

Valentin (falling).   Oh, agony!

Mephistopheles.   Now that lout's tamed!
  But let's be off! We need to disappear at once:
  They are already screaming murder.
  I get on admirably with the police,
  But blood-crimes are another matter.   3715

Martha (at the window). Out there! Out there!

Gretchen (at the window).   Bring a light!

Martha (as before). They're quarreling and scuffling, shouting and
    fighting.

People. Someone's already dead!

Martha (coming outside). The murderers, have they escaped?

---

37.   A sword worn only as a decoration.

Gretchen (*coming outside*). Who's lying here?

People.   Your mother's son.   3720

Gretchen. Almighty God! What anguish!

Valentin. I'm dying! That's soon said
              And even sooner done.
              Why do you women stand and wail and cry?
              Come here and listen to me!   3725
              (*All gather around him.*)
              My Gretchen, see! You are still young
              And haven't got much sense at all;
              You've handled matters very badly.
              Let me advise you privately:
              Now that you have become a whore,   3730
              Go ply your trade in public.

Gretchen. My brother! Lord! What's this about?

Valentin. Let's leave the good Lord out of it.
              What's done is done, unfortunately;
              As these things go, so it will go.   3735
              You started secretly with *one*,
              Soon others too will want their turn,
              And when a dozen have enjoyed you,
              The whole town will demand your favors.

              At first, when shame is born,   3740
              She's brought into the world in secret,
              And the veil of night is drawn
              Over her head and ears;
              Yes, people want to murder her.
              But as she grows and swells with pride,   3745
              She bares her head even in daytime,
              Although she hasn't become any prettier.
              The uglier her face becomes,
              The more she seeks the light of day.

And truly, I foresee the time,   3750
When every decent citizen
Recoils from you, you dirty slut,
As from a corpse that carries plague.
And when they look you in the eye,
Your heart will quail inside you!   3755
You'll never wear a golden chain,
Nor stand at the altar in church again!
Never in a pretty lace collar
Will you enjoy a dance again!
But in some dark and wretched corner   3760
You'll hide among the beggars and cripples,
And, even if the Lord forgives you,
On earth you always will be damned!

Martha. Commend your soul to God's great mercy!
Don't burden it with blasphemy!   3765

Valentin. If I could get my hands on you,
You shameful, pandering, dried-up hag!
I'd know how to find absolution
For all my sins, and in full measure!

Gretchen. Brother! To what hellish torment—   3770

Valentin. Forget the tears, I tell you!
When you absolved yourself of honor,
You gave my heart the heaviest blow.
I shall pass through the sleep of death
To God, a soldier good and true. (*He dies.*)   3775

Cathedral

(*Service, with organ and choir. Gretchen in the midst
of many people. Evil Spirit behind Gretchen.*)

Evil Spirit. How different it was, Gretchen,
When you used to come here to the altar,

Still innocent,
Stammering a prayer
From the well-thumbed book,   3780
Half child's game,
Half God, in your heart!
Gretchen!
Where are your wits?
What sinful deed   3785
Is in your heart?
Are you praying for your mother's soul,
Which slept its way, because of you, to long, long torment?
Whose blood lies at your door?
Beneath your heart   3790
Isn't it already stirring, swelling,
Alarming both itself and you
With its foreboding presence?

Gretchen. Oh! Oh!
If I could just get rid of these thoughts   3795
That go back and forth in me
Against my will!

Choir.   Dies irae, dies illa
Solvet saeclum in favilla.[38]
(The organ sounds.)

Evil Spirit. His wrath seizes you!   3800
The trumpet sounds!
The graves are quaking!
And your heart,
Resurrected
From ashen quiet   3805
To fiery torture,
Arises, quaking.

---

38. "Day of wrath, that day / Shall dissolve the world in dust." The opening lines of the
medieval Latin hymn about the day of judgment. The Evil Spirit's following verses begin
to depict that day.

Gretchen. If I could only get away from here!
    I feel as if the organ
    Is choking me,   3810
    The choir undoing
    My very heart.

Choir.   *Judex ergo cum sedebit,*
    Quidquid latet adparebit,
    Nil inultum remanebit.[39]   3815

Gretchen. It seems so tight!
    The walls and pillars
    Are trapping me;
    The vault
    Is crushing me!—Air!   3820

Evil Spirit. Hide yourself! For sin and shame
    Will not stay hidden.
    Air? Light?
    Woe to you!

Choir.   *Quid sum miser tunc dicturus?*   3825
    Quem patronum rogaturus?
    Cum vix justus sit securus.[40]

Evil Spirit. The transfigured turn
    Their faces from you.
    The pure shrink from   3830
    Extending hands to you.
    Woe!

Choir.   *Quid sum miser tunc dicturus?*

Gretchen. Neighbor! Your smelling salts! *(She faints.)*

---

39. "Therefore when the judge shall sit, / Whatever is hidden will appear / Nothing will remain unpunished."

40. "What shall I, wretched one, say then? / What patron saint implore? / When even the just man is hardly secure."

Walpurgis Night[41]

> (*The Harz mountains, in the vicinity of Schierke*
> *and Elend.[42] Faust and Mephistopheles.*)

Mephistopheles. Aren't you longing for a broomstick?   3835
          A sturdy goat would do the trick quite nicely.
          We're still a long way from our destination.

Faust.   As long as I feel fresh and steady on my legs,
          This walking stick's enough for me.
          Why make the journey shorter?   3840
          To creep through labyrinthine valleys
          And then ascend this cliff,
          From which the spring forever bubbling plummets—
          That's the delight that seasons paths like this!
          Already spring is weaving through the birch trees,   3845
          And even the spruce begins to feel its presence;
          Will not our limbs, then, feel it too?

Mephistopheles. I really do not sense a hint of spring!
          It's pretty wintry in my body;
          Some frost and snow along the way would suit me fine.   3850
          How sadly there the red moon's waning disk
          Rises with its belated glow;
          It gives such feeble light that with each step
          You run into a tree or rock!
          Let me at least request a will-o'-the-wisp!   3855
          I see one there that's blazing merrily.
          Hey there! My friend! Please come and join us!
          Why flame like that so pointlessly?
          Be good enough to light our way up there!

Will-o'-the-Wisp. In awe of you, I hope I'll manage   3860
          To govern my erratic nature;
          Our course is usually quite crooked.

---

41.   See note to line 2590.

42.   Two towns in the Harz mountains. The word *Elend* means "misery."

Mephistopheles. Ah, you aspire to imitate mankind.
          Now, in the devil's name, go straight!
          Or I'll blow out your flickering life.   3865

Will-o'-the-Wisp. I see that you're the master of the house,
          And I am happy to oblige you.
          Remember though! Today this mountain's mad with magic,
          And if you want a will-o'-the-wisp to guide you,
          You can't be overly particular.   3870

Faust, Mephistopheles, and the Will-o'-the-Wisp (in alternating song).
          We have entered, so it seems,
          The realm of magic and of dreams.
          Guide us well and earn our praises,
          That we may make rapid progress
          Through these wide and barren spaces!   3875

          Watch the trees behind the trees,
          See how quickly they move past us,
          And the cliffs that bow down low,
          And the jutting craggy noses,
          How they snore and how they blow!   3880

          Through the rocks and through the grasses
          Stream and brook are rushing down.
          Is it murmuring, is it singing,
          Is it love's lament I hear—
          Voices of those heavenly days?   3885
          All we hope for, all we love!
          And the echo, like a tale
          Of old times, resounds once more.

          Toowhit! Toowoo! Right in my ear,
          Screech-owl, peewit, screaming jay,   3890
          Can they all have stayed awake?
          Are those newts there in the bushes?
          Sprawling legs, distended bellies!
          And the tree-roots, like long snakes,
          Wind their way through rock and sand,   3895

Stretching their fantastic coils
Out to scare us and to catch us;
Stretching wriggling tentacles
Out from earthy growths and gnarls
Toward the traveler. And the mice, 3900
Multicolored, teeming, thronging
Through the moss and through the heather!
And the flashing glowworms fly,
Swarming by in tight formation,
A disorienting escort. 3905

Tell me, though, if we're at rest,
Or if we are moving forwards;
Everything, it seems, is spinning—
Cliffs and trees, all making faces,
And the wandering lights, inflating, 3910
Bursting, and proliferating.

Mephistopheles. Grab the corner of my cloak!
Here's a peak of medium height:
With astonishment you'll see
Mammon glowing deep inside it. 3915

Faust.   How strangely in the mountain's depths
A hazy light, like dawn's first red,
Appears to gleam! It shimmers even
In the deepest chasms of the abyss.
There vapors rise, there fumes are drifting, 3920
Here light glows from the misty veil,
Now trickling in a slender thread,
Now gushing in a fountain;
Here in a hundred veins it winds
Its way along the valley, 3925
And here in a tight corner
Becomes a single stream.
Meanwhile, bright sparks spray all around,
Like scattered grains of golden sand.
And see! From top to bottom now 3930
The cliff-face catches fire.

Mephistopheles. Lord Mammon is illuminating
        His palace brilliantly in honor of the feast.
        How fortunate that you have seen it;
        I sense unruly guests are on the way.   3935

Faust.   How the whirlwind rushes through the air!
        And with what blows it strikes my neck!

Mephistopheles. Grab hold of the ancient ribs of this cliff,
        Or you'll be tossed down to the chasm's crypt.
        Thick fog condenses the night.   3940
        Listen to the wind crashing through the forest!
        Startled, the owls fly off.
        Listen! Pillars are splintering
        In palaces of evergreen.
        Branches creaking and breaking!   3945
        Trunks droning with all their might!
        Roots rasping and tearing!
        In dreadful disorder they fall,
        Crashing down on one another,
        And through the gaping ruins   3950
        Gusts hiss and howl.
        Do you hear voices high above us?
        In the distance and nearby?
        Yes, a raging song of magic
        Is streaming all along the mountain!   3955

Witches (in chorus). The witches travel toward the Brocken,
        The stubble is yellow, the grain is green.
        The great horde is assembling there;
        Lord Urian[43] sits at the summit.
        We travel over sticks and stones,   3960
        The old witch farts, the billy-goat stinks.

---

43. A Low German name for the devil, from *Urhans* or "Old Jack."

Voice.	Old Baubo is arriving now,[44]
	She comes here riding on a sow.

Witches (chorus).	Honor to whom honor is due!
	Frau Baubo in front! Please lead her in! 3965
	A prodigious pig with Mother on it,
	Is followed by the horde of witches.

Voice.   Which way did you come?

Voice.	Over the Ilsenstein.[45]
	There I peeked into an owl's nest.
	She stared wide-eyed at me!

Voice.	Oh go to the devil! 3970
	Why must you ride so fast!

Voice.	She skinned my side as she rushed by;
	Just look at the gash she's given me!

Witches (chorus).	The way is broad, the way is long,
	What sort of furious crush is this? 3975
	The pitchfork stabs, the besom pricks,
	The mother bursts, the child's stillborn.

Warlocks (half-chorus).

We creep along like snails in their shells;
The women are all miles ahead.
For on the path to the evil one's house,   3980
Woman is way ahead of us.

---

44.   Robert Graves, *The Greek Myths* (London: Folio Society, 1996), vol. 1, p. 96: "Iambe and Baubo personify the obscene songs, in iambic metre, which were sung to relieve emotional tension at the Eleusinian Mysteries; but Iambe, Demeter, and Baubo form the familiar triad of maiden, nymph, and crone."

45.   The Ilsenstein is a high rock a few miles northeast of the Blocksberg or Brocken. (See note to line 2113.)

Warlocks (second half-chorus). That doesn't bother us at all,
　　　For while a woman makes her way
　　　With countless busy little steps,
　　　A man gets there with one great leap.   3985

Voice (up above). Come along, come along, from the rock-bound lake!

Voices (down below). We'd love to join you way up there;
　　　We're bathing and we're very pure,
　　　Though we're eternally infertile.

Both choruses. The wind is still, the stars have fled,   3990
　　　The hazy moon is trying to hide.
　　　The magic chorus, whizzing by,
　　　Sprays many thousand sparks of fire.

Voice (from below). Whoa there! Whoa!

Voice (from above). Who's calling from the rocky crevice?   3995

Voice (below). Take me along! Take me along!
　　　I've climbed three hundred years or more
　　　And cannot reach the summit there.
　　　I would so like to join my kind.

Both choruses. A broom will bear you, a cane will do;   4000
　　　A pitchfork will bear you, a goat will too;
　　　If you can't raise yourself today
　　　Then you are lost eternally.

Halfwitch (below). I've scurried after them so long;
　　　How did they get so far ahead?   4005
　　　I can't get peace and quiet at home
　　　And see I won't get any here.

Witches (chorus). This ointment gives us witches courage,
　　　A rag suffices for a sail,

And any trough serves as a boat.   4010
If not today, you'll never fly.

Both choruses. And as we draw close to the summit,
Skim slowly down toward the ground
And spread your coveys of witch-kind
Over the heath, far and wide.   4015
(*They descend.*)

Mephistopheles. They push and shove, they rustle and clatter!
They hiss and swirl, they pull and prattle!
They glow and spark and stink and burn!
The witches in their element!
Stay close to me, or we shall soon be parted.   4020
Where are you?

Faust (in the distance).   Over here!

Mephistopheles.   So far away already?
I'll have to show who's master of this house.
Make way! Squire Voland[46] comes. Make way, sweet rabble!
Here, Doctor, hold on tight! And we'll escape this mob
In a *single* bound;   4025
It's too insane, yes, even for the likes of me.
Right there I see a strange light gleaming,
And something draws me to those bushes,
Come here! We'll slip in there.

Faust.   Spirit of contradiction! Go ahead! Lead on!   4030
But really, this was awfully clever:
We've climbed the Brocken on Walpurgis Night,
Only to seek seclusion now we're here.

Mephistopheles. There, look at those bright flames!
A lively club is congregating.   4035
Where a few are gathered, one is not alone.

---

46. A name for the devil, from the Middle High German *vâlant*, or devil.

Faust.   But I'd much rather be up there!
           I see the glowing light and swirling smoke.
           The crowd streams toward the Evil One,
           And many a riddle is solved up there.   4040

Mephistopheles. But many a riddle is set as well.
           Just let the great world rush along,
           We'll settle down here where it's quiet.
           It is an old tradition, after all,
           To generate small worlds within the great.   4045
           I see young witches there bare naked;
           The old ones wisely keep their bodies covered.
           Be friendly, please, if only for my sake;
           The effort's small, the fun is great.
           I hear the noise of instruments!   4050
           Damned grating noise! It takes a bit of getting used to.
           Come along! Come along! You can't get out of it:
           I'll lead the way and introduce you,
           And you'll feel newly bound to me.
           What do you say, my friend? It's no small space.   4055
           Why just look there! It's hard to see the end of it.
           A hundred fires are burning in a row;
           They're dancing, chatting, cooking, drinking, making love;
           Now tell me, where could you find something better?

Faust.   And will you choose, by way of introduction,   4060
           To play the magician's or the devil's part?

Mephistopheles. It's true that I've grown used to traveling incognito,
           But on a gala day one must display one's order.
           I haven't the distinction of a garter,
           But here my cloven hoof is recognized and honored.   4065
           You see that snail there? Crawling this way
           With probing eyes,
           It has already sniffed me out.
           I can't conceal my identity here.
           But come! We'll go from fire to fire: 4070
           I'll do the wooing; you are the suitor.
                (To several who are seated around dying embers.)

Old gentlemen, why are you sitting way back here?
I'd praise you, if I found you in the midst
Of youthful riot and debauchery—
There's solitude enough at home.   4075

General. Why put your trust in nations?
It doesn't matter what you've done for them;
The populace, just like the ladies,
Gives precedence to younger men.

Minister. People have lost all sense of what is right.   4080
I laud the good old men of my day;
As long as we were in control,
That truly was the golden age.

Parvenu. If truth be told we weren't fools either,
And often did things we should not have;   4085
But nowadays the world is topsy-turvy,
Just when we'd like to keep it as it was.

Author. These days who will read anything
That's reasonably intelligent?
As for the younger generation,   4090
It's never been so insolent.

Mephistopheles (*who suddenly appears very old*).
On this my last climb up the witches' mountain,
I feel that men are ripe for Judgment Day;
And since my little cask is running cloudy,
I'm sure the world itself is running dry.   4095

Peddler-Witch. Please, gentlemen, don't just rush by!
Don't miss this opportunity!
Examine my wares carefully—
You'll find all kinds of things.
No shop on earth can rival mine,   4100
For there is nothing in it
That has not at some point inflicted

Real damage on the world and humankind—
No dagger here that has not dripped with blood,
No cup from which a caustic poison has not poured   4105
Into a sound and healthy body,
No jewel that has not led an honest woman
Astray, no sword that has not broken an alliance
Or stabbed an adversary from behind.

Mephistopheles. Dear auntie, you are way behind the times.   4110
What's done is gone! What's gone is done!
Invest in newer things instead!
Only the latest thing attracts us.

Faust.   I only hope I don't forget myself!
Now this is what I call a fair!   4115

Mephistopheles. The maelstrom strives and struggles to ascend;
You think you're pushing when you're being pushed.

Faust.   But who is that?

Mephistopheles.   Observe her closely!
That is Lilith.

Faust.   Who?

Mephistopheles.   Adam's first wife.
Beware of her beautiful hair: 4120
She likes to flaunt her one and only ornament,
And once she's caught a man with it,
She won't soon let him go again.

Faust.   That old crone and the young witch sitting there—
Those two were skipping energetically!   4125

Mephistopheles. There is no time for rest today.
Another dance is starting; come, we'll join them!

Faust (dancing with the young witch).
    One time I had a lovely dream,
    In which I saw an apple tree;
    And on that tree two apples shone—   4130
    They tempted me and I climbed up.

Pretty Witch. You've craved those little apples so,
    Since you were first in paradise.
    I feel transported with delight,
    To think my garden bears such fruit.   4135

Mephistopheles (with the old witch).
    One night I had a juicy dream,
    In which I saw a cloven tree
    And in that tree a [monstrous hole];[47]
    [Big] as it was, I found it pleasing.

Old Witch. Let me extend my humble greetings   4140
    To the noble knight of the cloven hoof!
    Make sure you've got a [decent stopper],
    Unless you're frightened by [big holes].

Proktophantasmist.[48] Damned people! How presumptuous you are!
    Was it not demonstrated long ago   4145
    That spirits never stand on proper feet?
    And now you even dance the way we humans do!

Pretty Witch (dancing). What does he want here at our party?

Faust (dancing). Oh him! He's everywhere these days.
    Where others dance, there he must criticize.   4150
    If there's a step on which he can't expound at length,

---

47. The bracketed words are in the manuscript, but dashes were substituted in all the printed editions.

48. The meaning is clear enough: the Greek noun *prōktos* means anus. The satire is directed at Friedrich Nicolai, a rationalist critic and writer who wrote a parody of Goethe's first novel, *The Sorrows of Young Werther.*

That step's as good as non-existent.
He's most incensed when we move forwards.
If you'd agree to go in circles,
The way he does in his old mill,   4155
He'd like that somewhat better—
Especially if you'd first consult him on the matter.

Proktophantasmist. What, you're still there! No, that's outrageous.
    Just disappear! We've spread enlightenment!
    These devils don't play by the rules.   4160
    For all our cleverness, there are still ghosts in Tegel.[49]
    How long have I been sweeping out illusions—
    Things get no cleaner; it's outrageous!

Pretty Witch. Then stop and don't get on our nerves!

Proktophantasmist. I'll tell you spirits to your faces,   4165
    I won't put up with spiritual despotism;
    My spirit cannot tolerate it.[50]
    (*The dancing continues.*)
    I am not making any progress here today,
    Although I benefit from all my travels
    And hope, before I take my final step,   4170
    To subjugate all poets and all devils.

Mephistopheles. He'll sit down in some puddle now,
    For that's how he relieves his pain;
    When leeches banquet on his buttocks,
    He's cured of spirits and of spirit.   4175
      (*To Faust, who has withdrawn from the dance.*)
    Why did you let her go, that lovely girl,
    Who sang so sweetly while you danced?

Faust. Oh! In the middle of her song
    A red mouse jumped out of her mouth.

---

49.   Near Berlin. In 1797 a Berlin paper reported a nocturnal ruckus there, which many attributed to a ghost.

50.   Alternately, "My mind can't tolerate it." It is helpful to remember here that the German word *Geist* means "mind" or "intellect" as well as "spirit."

Mephistopheles. Why, that's alright! Don't be too finicky!   4180
    Be glad the mouse was not a common grey one.
    Who cares about such details in idyllic hours?

Faust. Then I saw—

Mephistopheles.   What?

Faust.   Mephisto, do you see
    A pale and lovely child that stands alone far from the rest?
    Slowly she drags herself along;   4185
    She seems to be walking with fettered feet.
    I must admit it seems to me
    That she resembles my good Gretchen.

Mephistopheles. Leave that alone! It won't help anyone.
    It is a magic image, lifeless; it's an idol.   4190
    It isn't good to come upon it;
    Its frozen gaze makes human blood congeal
    And almost turns a man to stone—
    I'm sure you've heard of the Medusa.

Faust. It's true, they are a corpse's eyes,   4195
    Eyes that no loving hand has closed.
    That is the breast that Gretchen offered me;
    That's the sweet body I enjoyed.

Mephistopheles. But that is magic, credulous fool!
    To everyone she looks just like his darling.   4200

Faust. What bliss! What agony!
    I cannot leave this vision.
    How curiously her lovely throat's adorned
    By a single thin red string
    No wider than a knife-blade!   4205

Mephistopheles. Quite right! I see it too.
    At times she carries her head in her arms—

Perseus cut it off.
You're still delighted by illusions!
But come up this small hill with me,   4210
It's as delightful here as in the Prater;[51]
And if I'm not deceived,
I really see a theater.
What's going on?

Servibilis. They are about to start again.
This is the newest play, the last of seven;   4215
It is our custom to put on that many.
A dilettante has written it,
And dilettantes perform it too.
Excuse me, gentlemen, I have to disappear:
It's my delight to raise the curtain.   4220

Mephistopheles. I'm glad to find you on the Blocksberg,
Because that's just where you belong.

Walpurgis Night's Dream, or the Golden Anniversary of Oberon and Titania[52]

  Intermezzo.

Stage Manager. We can take a rest today,
Stalwart sons of Mieding.[53]
Ancient peak and misty valley   4225
Are all the props they'll need!

Herald. Golden anniversary
Means fifty years are over;
When man and wife are reconciled—
That golden is far dearer.   4230

---

51. An amusement park in Vienna.

52. Oberon and Titania are the king and queen of the fairies in Shakespeare's *A Midsummer Night's Dream.* Their quarrel and reconciliation are central to the action of that play.

53. Mieding was a carpenter and stage manager at the Weimar court theater. He died in 1782.

Oberon. If you spirits are with me,
    Now's the hour to show it,
    For the king and his dear queen
    Are once more united.

Puck.[54] Puck is here and twirls around,   4235
    Sliding his feet in the dance;
    Behind him come a hundred more
    To join the merriment.

Ariel.[55] Ariel intones his song
    In pure celestial sounds;   4240
    His melody lures homely faces,
    But draws the pretty ladies too.

Oberon. Spouses who would live in concord,
    Learn a lesson from us!
    To make two people love each other,   4245
    You need only part them.

Titania. When husbands grouse and wives have fancies,
    Just seize them both adeptly;
    Lead her to equatorial climes
    And him to northern regions.   4250

Full Orchestra (fortissimo). Snout of fly and nose of gnat
    And all that's of that genre,
    Frog and cricket in the grass—
    Such are our musicians!

Solo. And see, the bagpipe's coming there!   4255
    Soap-bubble is his name.
    Note the droning monotone
    That blows through his snub nose.

---

54. Puck is the mischievous elf who plays an important role in *A Midsummer Night's Dream*.

55. Ariel is the airy spirit and songster of Shakespeare's *The Tempest*.

Spirit in the Process of Formation. A spider's foot, a toad's round belly,
  Some wings for the tiny thing!   4260
  They won't produce a living creature,
  But they will make a verse.

A Tiny Couple. A little step, a lofty leap
  Through honeyed dew and breezes;
  Although you've tripped me up a lot,   4265
  We can't get off the ground.

Curious Traveler. Tell me it's not just a costume!
  I don't believe my eyes—
  Can it be Oberon I see,
  That handsome god, here today?   4270

Orthodox Person. Without a claw, without a tail!
  Yet there's no doubt about it:
  Just like the gods of ancient Greece,
  He too is a real devil.

Northern Artist. What I can capture here today   4275
  Is really pretty sketchy;
  But I am getting ready now
  For my Italian journey.

Purist. Alas, an ill fate leads me on:
  What disgraceful habits!   4280
  In this great company of witches
  Only two wear powder.

Young Witch. Like a skirt your powder suits
  A grey and bent old crone;
  I'll sit stark naked on my goat,   4285
  Exhibiting my body.

Matron. We're far too well-bred and refined
  To pout or show displeasure,

Yet young and tender as you are,
I hope you'll putrefy!   4290

Conductor. Snout of fly and nose of gnat,
        Don't swarm the naked lady!
        Frog and cricket in the grass,
        Please try to keep the rhythm!

Weather-Vane (pointing to one side). The very society one wants.   4295
        Prospective brides all over!
        And bachelors who to a man
        Are people full of promise!

Weather-Vane (pointing to the other side). And if the earth does not
            split open
        And swallow all of them,   4300
        Then let me take a running start
        And jump straight down to hell.

Xenia.[56] We've come here now as biting insects,
        With pincers small but sharp,
        To worship, as is right and meet,   4305
        Satan, lord and father.

Hennings.[57] See how they crowd and throng and joke
        Naively with each other!
        And in the end they'll even claim
        That it was all good-hearted.   4310

Musaget.[58] I'd really like to disappear
        Here among these witches;

---

56.   The name given to Goethe and Schiller's satirical distichs published in 1797. "Xenia"
means "gifts for guests"; here, the Xenia present themselves as gadflies.

57.   August von Hennings (1746–1826) was a minor literary figure who, in his journal,
The Genius of the Age, had attacked some of Goethe and Schiller's publications.

58.   I.e., "leader of the muses." The name is the title of another of Hennings' publications.

Frankly, I could lead them on
More easily than muses.

Ci-devant Genius of the Age.[59] With the right sort you'll get
        somewhere.   4315
    Come, hang on to my coattails!
    The Blocksberg has a spacious summit,
    Like the German Parnassus.[60]

Curious Traveler. Say, what's the name of that stiff man?
    He walks with haughty steps.   4320
    He sniffs whatever he can sniff.
    "He's tracking Jesuits."

Crane.[61] I like to fish where things are clear,
    In cloudy waters too;
    That's why you see this pious man   4325
    Mingling with these devils.

Child of the World. Yes, for pious folk, believe me,
    All things are vehicles;
    And even on the Blocksberg here,
    They'll form conventicles.   4330

A Dancer. That must be some new chorus coming?
    I hear a distant drumming.

---

59. I.e., "former genius of the age." A reference to Hennings' journal, but also an allusion to the term *ci-devant nobles,* used during and after the French Revolution to refer to aristocrats whose titles had been revoked.

60. Mount Parnassus is the mountain in central Greece that was the traditional home of the Muses. The suggestion is that the "German Parnassus" can accommodate almost any poet who writes in German.

61. In 1829 Goethe spoke about the Swiss preacher and physiognomist Johann Kaspar Lavater: "Strict truth was not really his thing; he deceived himself and others.... He walked like a crane, and therefore appears as a crane on the Blocksberg." Johann Peter Eckermann, *Gespräche mit Goethe in den letzten Jahren seines Lebens* (Leipzig: Brockhaus, 1837), vol. 2, p. 70 (conversation of February 17, 1829; my translation).

Don't worry! In the reeds the bitterns
Thrum in unison.

Dance-Master. Each lifts his legs and extricates   4335
Himself as best he can!
The bent ones jump; the clumsy hop—
They don't care what it looks like.

Fiddler. Those rogues abhor each other so,
Each longs to do the other in;   4340
As Orpheus' lyre subdued the beasts,
The bagpipe here unites them.

Dogmatist. I will not let critiques and doubts
Drive me to distraction.
It's clear the devil must exist—   4345
How else could there be devils?

Idealist. Inside my mind, imagination
Is all too domineering:
For if I really am all this,
Then clearly I am raving.   4350

Realist. Essence is what troubles me,
And it disturbs me deeply;
For the first time I find that I'm
Unsteady on my feet.

Supernaturalist. I'm just delighted to be here;   4355
I'll celebrate with these;
For from these devils I deduce
The existence of good spirits.

Skeptic. They're tracking tiny sparks of light,
And think they're near the treasure.   4360
'Devil' sounds a lot like 'doubtful,'
And doubt is my *métier.*

Conductor. Frog and cricket in the grass!
    Dilettantes be damned!
    Snout of fly and nose of gnat,   4365
    I thought you were musicians!

The Adept. Sanssouci[62] is what they call
    This troop of merry creatures;
    We can't walk on our feet these days,
    So we go on our heads.   4370

The Inept.[63] We used to get on by bowing and scraping,
    But Heaven help us now!
    We've scraped right through the soles of our shoes
    And have to wander barefoot.

Will-o'-the-Wisps. From the bogs and swamps we come,   4375
    Where we were engendered;
    But dance on equal footing here,
    Flamboyant men about town.

Shooting Star. From on high I shot down here
    In a burst of starry fire,   4380
    Now I lie twisted in the grass—
    Who'll help me to my feet?

Massive Ones.[64] Make room, make room, on all sides please!
    That's how the grass gets trampled,
    Spirits gather; spirits too   4385
    Have rather clumsy limbs.

---

62. I.e., *sans souci*, French, meaning "without care." Sanssouci is the name of the palace outside Berlin built by Frederick the Great between 1745 and 1747. "The Adept" probably refers to the opportunists who—without scruples—changed their political leanings after the French Revolution.

63. Less successful émigrés of the French Revolution, although the satire in this quatrain and the following ones should not be regarded as aimed only at the French.

64. Possibly a reference to the masses empowered by the French Revolution.

Puck. Don't come on stage with lumbering feet
　　　Like baby elephants!
　　　May the clumsiest one today
　　　Be earthy Puck himself.   4390

Ariel. If loving nature gave you wings,
　　　If the spirit gave them,
　　　Follow my light traces now,
　　　Up to the hill of roses!

Orchestra (pianissimo). Trailing clouds and veils of fog   4395
　　　Are melting into air.
　　　A breeze in the leaves and wind in the reeds,
　　　And everything dissolves.

Dreary Day, Field[65]

(Faust and Mephistopheles.)

Faust. Wretched! In despair! Wandering pitiably over the face of the earth for so long and now caught! Locked in prison as a criminal to suffer appalling tortures—that gentle unhappy creature! That far! That far! Treacherous, contemptible spirit, and this you concealed from me! Yes, stand, just stand there! Roll your diabolical eyes furiously around in your head! Stand and defy me with your unbearable presence! Caught! Wretched beyond recall! Handed over to evil spirits and judging, unfeeling mankind! And in the meantime you lull me with vulgar diversions, hide her growing misery from me, and let her go helplessly to ruin!

Mephistopheles. She's not the first.

Faust. Dog! Abominable monster! Change him, infinite Spirit! Change this worm back into his dog-form—the way he used to trot along in front

---

65. This scene is written in prose and the lines are not numbered. The earliest version of *Faust*, written between 1772 and 1775, contained a number of scenes in prose, which Goethe later revised and versified. At that time he decided to leave this scene in its original form and made only a few slight changes to it. The abrupt shift in tone clearly signals that we have left the magical realm of Walpurgis Night.

of me at night, roll at the feet of an unsuspecting traveler, and jump on his shoulders as he tripped and fell. Change him back into his favorite shape and let him crawl on his belly in the sand in front of me, so I can step on him, the reprobate! Not the first! Misery! Misery! No human soul can grasp that more than one creature sank to such depths of wretchedness, that the first was not enough to atone for the guilt of all the rest, as she writhed in mortal agony before the eyes of the One who forgives eternally! The wretchedness of this one girl eats at my marrow and my very life; you grin casually at the fate of thousands!

Mephistopheles. We're already at the end of our wits again, at the point where you people lose your minds. Why do you associate with us, if you can't endure it? You want to fly and are afraid of heights? Did we thrust ourselves on you, or you on us?

Faust. Don't bare your greedy teeth at me like that! You disgust me! Great and glorious spirit,[66] you who deigned to appear to me, you who know my very heart and soul, why must you weld me to this shameful companion, who feeds on harm and finds refreshment in ruin?

Mephistopheles. Are you almost done?

Faust. Rescue her! Or woe to you! The most dreadful curse on you for millennia!

Mephistopheles. I cannot undo the bonds of the avenger; I cannot open his latches. Rescue her! Who threw her down into ruin? Me, or you?

(*Faust looks wildly around.*)

Mephistopheles. Are you reaching for some thunder? A good thing it wasn't given to you wretched mortals! By annihilating an innocent opponent— that's how a tyrant vents his rage in such predicaments.

Faust. Take me there! She shall be free!

---

66.   Faust seems to be appealing to the Earth Spirit, although there is no prior indication in our text that this Spirit has power over Mephistopheles.

Mephistopheles. And the danger you'll expose yourself to? Remember, the blood your hand shed still defiles the city.[67] Avenging spirits hover over the site of the murder and lie in wait for the murderer who returns.

Faust. This too from you? The murder and death of the world be upon you, monster! Take me there, I tell you, and set her free!

Mephistopheles. I'll take you, but listen to what I can do! Do I hold all power in heaven and on earth? I'll befog the guard's senses—you get hold of his keys and lead her out of there with your human hand! I'll keep watch! The magic horses are ready; I'll carry you both away. That I can do.

Faust. Up and away!

Night, Open Field

> (*Faust and Mephistopheles rushing by on black horses.*)

Faust.   Why are they weaving about over on the Rabenstein?[68]

Mephistopheles. I don't know what they're cooking up and doing
over there.   4400

Faust.   They drift up, drift down, bow their heads, and kneel.

Mephistopheles. A coven of witches.

Faust.   They're scattering something and consecrating it.

Mephistopheles. Onward! Onward!

---

67. Mephistopheles is referring to the murder of Valentin.

68. I.e., "Ravenstone." This was the name of the site of execution outside the walls of the city of Frankfurt.

Prison

Faust (with a bundle of keys and a lamp, in front of a small iron door).
    A long-forgotten shuddering comes over me;   4405
    I'm overcome by all the misery of mankind.
    She lives behind this damp wall here—
    A good illusion was her only crime!
    You hesitate to go to her!
    You're afraid to see her again!   4410
    Go! Your misgivings only drag death closer. *(He grasps the lock.)*

Voice (singing inside).
    My mother, the whore,
    Who murdered me!
    My father, the rascal,
    Who ate me up!   4415
    My little sister
    Gathered the bones
    In a shady spot;
    Then I became a pretty little wood-bird;
    Fly away, fly away!   4420

Faust (unlocking the door). She doesn't sense that her beloved is listening
    And hears the chains clank, the straw that rustles.
    (He enters.)

Margarete (hiding on her mattress).
    Oh! Oh! They're coming. Bitter death!

Faust (softly). Quiet! Quiet! I've come to free you.

Margarete (writhing before him).
    If you are human, feel my need.   4425

Faust.   You'll shout the guards out of their sleep!
    (He takes hold of the chains in order to unlock them.)

Margarete (on her knees). Hangman, who has given you
    This power over me!

You've come to get me and it's only midnight.
Be merciful and let me live!   4430
Isn't tomorrow morning soon enough?
   (*She stands up.*)
And I am still so young, so young!
And have to die so soon!
I was pretty too, and that was my undoing.
Near was my friend, now he is far away;[69]   4435
Torn is the wreath, the flowers are scattered.
Don't seize me with such violence!
Spare me! What have I done to you?
Don't let me supplicate in vain,
I've never seen you in my life!   4440

Faust.   Will I survive this misery?

Margarete. I'm wholly in your power now.
   Just let me nurse the child before I go.
   I held her close all night;
   They took her from me to torment me,   4445
   And now they say I murdered her.
   I'll never be happy again.
   And they sing songs to mock me! It's wicked of people!
   There's an old tale that ends like that—
   Who asked them what it means?   4450

Faust (throwing himself down). A lover is lying at your feet;
   I've come to unlock the chains of misery.

Margarete (throwing herself beside him).
   O let us kneel and call upon the saints!
   See! Beneath these steps,
   Beneath the doorsill,   4455
   Hell is seething!

---

69.   Both here and in the following Gretchen refers to Faust as her "friend" (*Freund*), evoking both Luther's and Goethe's German translations of the Song of Solomon. For example, both Luther and Goethe render Song of Solomon 2:8, which Gretchen echoes in line 4461, as "the voice of my friend." (For Goethe's translation, see WA, part I, vol. 37, p. 306.)

With dreadful fury,
The Evil One
Is making a din!

Faust (loudly). Gretchen! Gretchen!   4460

Margarete (attentively). That was the voice of my friend!
   (She jumps up. Her chains fall off.)
  Where is he? I heard him calling.
  I'm free! No one shall stop me.
  I want to fly into his arms,
  To lie upon his breast!   4465
  He called, "Gretchen!" He stood in the doorway.
  In the midst of the weeping and gnashing of hell,
  Through the furious, devilish scorn,
  I recognized that sweet and loving tone.

Faust. It's me!

Margarete.   It's you! Oh say it one more time!   4470
  (She holds him.)
  It's him! It's him! Where is all torment now?
  Where is my fear of prison and of chains?
  It's you! You've come to save me!
  I am saved!
  And now the street is there again,   4475
  Where I first saw you.
  And the cheerful garden,
  Where Martha and I are waiting for you.

Faust (urging her along). Come with me! Come!

Margarete.   Oh stay a while!
  For I so love to stay with you.   4480
  (Caressing him.)

Faust. Hurry!
  If you don't hurry,
  We'll pay for it dearly.

Margarete. What? You can't kiss any more?
    My friend, away so briefly, 4485
    And you've forgotten how to kiss?
    Why do I feel so frightened in your arms?
    When every word of yours, each glance,
    Used to overwhelm me with a heaven.
    And you would almost suffocate me with your kisses. 4490
    Kiss me!
    Or I'll kiss you!
      (*She embraces him.*)
    Oh! Your lips are cold,
    Are dumb.
    Where has your love 4495
    Gone?
    Who took it from me?
      (*She turns away from him.*)

Faust. Come! Follow me! Darling, take heart!
    I'll hold you close with thousandfold passion;
    Just follow me! That's all I ask! 4500

Margarete (*turning toward him*).
    Then is it you? And is it really you?

Faust. It is! Come with me!

Margarete.   You're undoing my fetters,
    Taking me in your lap again.
    How is it that you aren't afraid of me?
    And do you know, my friend, who it is you free? 4505

Faust. Come! Come! Deep night begins to yield to dawn.

Margarete. I murdered my mother.
    I drowned my child.
    Was it not given to you and me?
    To you as well. It's you! I can hardly believe it. 4510
    Give me your hand! It's not a dream!

Your dear hand! Oh, but it's wet!
Wipe it off! It seems to me,
There's blood on it.
Oh God! What have you done!   4515
Put away your sword,
I beg you!

Faust.   Let bygones be bygones.
You're killing me.

Margarete. No, you must stay alive!   4520
I want to describe the graves to you.
You must see to them
Tomorrow;
You must give my mother the best place,
My brother right beside her;   4525
Set me a bit to the side,
But not too far!
And the little one at my right breast.
No one else will lie beside me!
To nestle close against your side,   4530
That was a sweet and gentle joy!
But I can't do it anymore;
It seems as if I have to force myself on you,
As if you're pushing me away;
And yet it's you, and you look so good, so true. 4535

Faust.   If you feel it's me, then come!

Margarete. Out there?

Faust.   Out there, to freedom.

Margarete.   If the grave's out there,
If death is lurking, then come!
From here to an eternal bed of rest—   4540
Not one step further—
You're leaving? Heinrich, if I could only go with you!

Faust. You can; just choose to! The door is open.

Margarete. I cannot leave; there is no hope for me.
　　　Why flee? They'll only lie in wait for me.　　4545
　　　It is so wretched to beg for a living,
　　　And with a guilty conscience too!
　　　It is so wretched to stray through foreign places,
　　　And anyway, they're sure to catch me!

Faust. I'll be there with you.　　4550

Margarete. Quick! Quick!
　　　Save your poor child.
　　　Go! Take the path
　　　Along the stream,
　　　Over the footbridge,　　4555
　　　Into the woods,
　　　On the left, by the plank,
　　　In the pond.
　　　Grab hold of her!
　　　She's trying to rise,　　4560
　　　She's still wriggling!
　　　Save her! Save her!

Faust. Come to your senses!
　　　Just *one* step, and you'll be free!

Margarete. If only we were past that hill!　　4565
　　　My mother sits there on a stone—
　　　A cold hand seems to be grabbing my hair!
　　　My mother sits there on a stone,
　　　And slowly wags her head;
　　　Not waving, not nodding, her head is too heavy;　　4570
　　　She slept so long, she'll wake no more.
　　　She slept, so we could enjoy ourselves.
　　　Those were such happy times!

Faust. If my entreaties and my words are of no use,
　　　I'll have to carry you away.　　4575

Margarete. Leave me! No, I'll suffer no violence!
　　　　Don't hold me so brutally!
　　　　I did everything else for love of you.

Faust.　Grey day is dawning! Darling! Darling!

Margarete. Day! Yes, day is breaking! The last day is closing in;　　4580
　　　　It was to have been my wedding day!
　　　　Tell no one you've already been with Gretchen.
　　　　Oh, my wreath!
　　　　But that's all over.
　　　　We'll see each other again—　　　　　　　　　　　　4585
　　　　But not at the dance.
　　　　The multitude crowds round; you cannot hear them.
　　　　The square, the streets
　　　　Can't hold them all.
　　　　The bell calls out, the white stick breaks.[70]　　　　4590
　　　　How they bind me and grip me!
　　　　They tie me to the execution-chair.
　　　　Now every neck feels the sharp blade
　　　　That's flashing toward my neck.
　　　　The world lies silent as the grave!　　　　　　　　4595

Faust.　If only I'd never been born!

Mephistopheles (appearing outside). Up! Or you're lost.
　　　　Useless delays! You hesitate, you talk!
　　　　My horses are shivering,
　　　　Morning is breaking.　　　　　　　　　　　　　　4600

Margarete. What's rising out of the ground?
　　　　Him! Him! Send him away!
　　　　What does he want in this sacred place?
　　　　He wants me!

---

70. Gretchen envisions her execution. A white stick was broken over the condemned prior to the beheading.

Faust.   You shall live!

Margarete. Judgment of God! I have given myself over to you!   4605

Mephistopheles (to Faust). Come! Come! Or I'll leave you there with her.

Margarete. I am yours, Father! Save me!
     You angels! You holy hosts,
     Camp round about me and preserve me![71]
     Heinrich! You fill me with dread.   4610

Mephistopheles. She is condemned!

Voice (from above).   Is saved!

Mephistopheles (to Faust).   Come here to me!
     (Mephistopheles disappears with Faust.)

Voice (from within, fading away). Heinrich! Heinrich!

---

71.   Psalm 34:7.